"Stay away from him!" Damon snarled

"You've caused enough upset here!"

Kendra could scarcely believe what she was hearing. Damon was referring to Costas, his business partner's son, a flirtatious young man who seemed to have trouble staying away from *her*. Angrily she asked, "I've caused enough upset? How?"

"My partner has enough to worry about without you leading his son astray!" Damon went on furiously.

"Leading him astray?" Kendra choked. "He's twenty-two, the same age as me."

Damon took an angry step closer. "He might be the same age in years, Miss Jephcott, but you're years ahead in experience."

Kendra stood motionless for a numb moment, and then, as Damon moved inexorably nearer to her, she realized with a shock what he intended....

Jessica Steele first tried her hand at writing romance novels at her husband's encouragement two years after they were married. She fondly remembers the day her first novel was accepted for publication. "Peter mopped me up, and neither of us cooked that night," she recalls. "We went out to dinner." She and her husband live in a hundred-year-old cottage in Worcestershire, and they've traveled to many fascinating places—such as China, Japan, Mexico and Denmark—that make wonderful settings for her books.

Books by Jessica Steele

HARLEQUIN ROMANCE

2687—NO HONOURABLE COMPROMISE
2789—MISLEADING ENCOUNTER
2800—SO NEAR, SO FAR
2850—BEYOND HER CONTROL
2861—RELATIVE STRANGERS
2916—UNFRIENDLY ALLIANCE
2928—FORTUNES OF LOVE
2964—WITHOUT LOVE
2982—WHEN THE LOVING STOPPED

HARLEQUIN PRESENTS

717—RUTHLESS IN ALL
725—GALLANT ANTAGONIST
749—BOND OF VENGEANCE
766—NO HOLDS BARRED
767—FACADE
836—A PROMISE TO DISHONOUR

TO STAY FOREVER

Jessica Steele

Harlequin Books

TORONTO • NEW YORK • LONDON
AMSTERDAM • PARIS • SYDNEY • HAMBURG
STOCKHOLM • ATHENS • TOKYO • MILAN

Original hardcover edition published in 1989
by Mills & Boon Limited

ISBN 0-373-03011-8

Harlequin Romance first edition October 1989

Printed in U.S.A.

CHAPTER ONE

THE 707 left Gatwick and soared into the night sky. Shortly afterwards the 'Fasten Seat Belts' sign went off. Kendra relaxed. It was the first time she'd had the chance of such a luxury during the last couple of days.

'Thank you,' she murmured to the pretty stewardess who in no time at all, it seemed, was there to present her with her meal tray. Kendra undid the tinfoil of the heated portion of her pre-packed dinner and, as the heady smell of a common or garden stew assailed her nostrils, she only then realised just how ravenous she was. Come to think of it, she mused, as she got busy with her fork, if there had been no time to relax, then neither had there been time to eat; well, nothing that was in any way substantial, anyhow. It had been all go ever since Aunt Heather had telephoned the office yesterday.

Tucking into the gravyless stew with as much relish as if it was caviare, Kendra had time then to feel faintly incredulous that, up until two days ago, she hadn't had so much as one thought in her head about flying to Greece tonight. In fact, before her mother's telephone call on Wednesday her thoughts had been more on what was she going to do about her present boyfriend—who was showing all the signs of getting serious.

She had been in the middle of pondering what she would do about Nigel when the phone in the flat which she shared with Janice had rung.

Janice was, reluctantly, away on a five-day course in connection with her job. Janice, though, was not a good mixer, and Kendra, suspecting that her friend and flatmate might start to feel fed up around mid-week, had suggested that she ring up for a chat if she felt lonely.

Fully expecting to have to do a cheer-up job on Janice, Kendra had discovered on answering the phone that her services in that department were not required. For Janice, presumably getting on better with her fellow course-attenders than she had anticipated, was not her caller.

'I didn't really expect to find you in on a Wednesday night!' Mary Jephcott, Kendra's mother, had opened cheerfully.

Kendra was extremely fond of her family, and had a smile of pleasure in her voice as she replied, 'You make it sound as though I'm always out.'

'I thought you usually went out on a Wednes... Ah!' Mrs Jephcott had said, suddenly seeing some light. 'It's happened again, hasn't it?'

'I... *what's* happened?' Kendra had asked.

She was sure that she had said nothing to her mother of her fear that Nigel was growing serious, so she was a little amazed when her mother answered, 'Like a few others in the past, this Nigel you've been seeing recently wants to go steady, doesn't he?'

Perceiving a trace of anxiety in her parent's tone, Kendra had swallowed her amazement to query carefully, 'Now why should the fact of Nigel Robinson, or anyone else, wanting to go steady bother me?'

'Apart from your natural sensitivity about hurting anyone, you've been backing away from anything remotely approaching a steady relationship ever since young Joey Miller went to pieces over you when you were in the sixth form together.'

'Mother!' Kendra gasped, amazed anew. 'That was five years ago!'

'I know that! Just as I know that, for all everyone tried to tell you that Joey having such a bad time just then had as much to do with him cramming for his exams as it had to do with you, it really knocked you sideways.'

'Oh,' Kendra murmured, and, realising that her mother must have been aware of how vulnerable she had been at seventeen, she decided to change the subject. 'So,' she said brightly, 'what else is new? Why did you ring when you thought I might be out tonight?' Her mother, she discovered, had not done with amazing her yet.

'How about—your cousin Faye is pregnant?'

Utterly astonished, not to say delighted, for she had not heard a word from her cousin since she had attended her wedding six months ago, Kendra gasped, 'Is she? How lovely! Oh, I must write to her—Aunt Heather will have her address, since Faye has written to tell her about the baby. I'll...'

'Faye hasn't written to her mother,' Kendra's parent quickly quashed that notion. 'Neither Heather nor Leslie have heard a word from her since Faye had that stand-up row with her father a year ago.'

Astounded that, in these new circumstances of Heather and Leslie Jephcott going to become grandparents, the breach had still not been healed, Kendra asked with yet more amazement, 'You mean Faye wrote and told you before she told her mother?'

'Faye hasn't told anyone and, if she hasn't written to you, she hasn't written to anyone either.'

'Then how...'

'How do I know that she's five months pregnant?' Kendra had still been taking in the fact that her lovely cousin was already five months pregnant and that this was the first they had heard about it when her mother cleared some of the confusion by telling her, 'Eugene Themelis, Heather's son-in-law, rang her from Greece.'

'Eugene rang Aunt Heather!' Kendra exclaimed, aware that her aunt had never met him, she herself being the only Jephcott who had been invited to the wedding.

Kendra was to swallow more and more surprise when, in the next few minutes, her mother outlined the contents of the wealthy Greek businessman's call to Faye's mother. For not only had Eugene acquainted his mother-in-law with the fact that her daughter was five months pregnant, but he had also invited his wife's parents to visit them in Greece.

'How super!' Kendra said without thinking. When she *had* thought for a moment, however, 'Will Uncle Leslie go, though?' she asked a shade doubtfully.

'Of course he won't!' her mother said in disgust. 'You know how stubborn he is! Faye has offended him, so *she* has to be the one to speak first. Which is a pity,' she went on, 'because Faye must be most unhappy at this present time.'

'Unhappy!' Kendra exclaimed. 'How do you make that out?' And, remembering the wedding and how Eugene had not been able to take his eyes off his lovely bride, she itemised, 'Eugene positively adores her, she has no money problems, and to crown that, she's having a baby.'

'Well, since Faye invited neither of her parents to the wedding, her husband must know that there's temporary bad blood flowing, so I can't think why else he would ring out of the blue asking them to pay her a visit.' She thought for a second and then put forward the notion, 'Perhaps she's homesick.'

Kendra came away from the phone having jokingly told her mother that she'd like half the chance to go to Greece and be homesick, but having seriously vetoed any suggestion that her cousin could be pining for England.

Going into the kitchen to make herself a cup of coffee, Kendra reflected on how she and Faye had been born and brought up in the small Worcestershire village of Barton Avery. With their two fathers being brothers and the families living in the same village, they had shared a good many outings. Faye was two years older than Kendra, but that didn't stop them being the best of companions. Both had attended the same dance class, though it was Faye who was the more gifted dancer.

Kendra poured hot water on the instant coffee in her cup and contemplated how she was fairly sure that her cousin was not homesick. She calculated that Faye must have been just sixteen on that evening when, as the two of them were returning from one of their dancing classes, Faye had confided, 'There's so much of the world I want to see—I just can't wait to shake the dust of Barton Avery off my heels.'

'You want to leave Barton Avery?' Kendra had recalled enquiring with wide-eyed wonder.

'Don't you!' her cousin had asked, looking horrified at the thought of anyone *choosing* to remain in the village.

'I—er—haven't thought about it,' she'd answered.

Only some years later, when Faye, using her talent to the full, had danced out of Barton Avery, and with some experience behind her had joined a touring troupe and had danced out of the country, did Kendra begin to get itchy feet herself.

She had held down the urge to go and find out what the world had to offer, though. Her parents would probably have had heart-failure if she had told them she was leaving the nest—say, for London. And anyhow, she was doing so well in her secretarial job that there was no earthly reason why she should move on. At least, that was what she had told herself for the next few months, and then Faye had returned briefly to England and had made one of her lightning visits home.

'My God, you're not still with that cruddy firm of solicitors, are you?' she had asked forthrightly.

In Kendra's view, Faye had grown a hard outer edge, but since she knew that deep down a softer person existed, she had smiled at her cousin's horror, and to her own surprise she had found herself confiding, 'To be honest, I *have* thought of looking for something more—exciting.'

'Do it,' Faye had urged. 'They're screaming out for secretaries in London.' She had then regaled Kendra with some of her exploits and had told her of some of the places she had seen, and Kendra, more unsettled than ever, had come closer and closer to throwing up her nice, safe but unexciting job.

Whether she would actually have given up her job and tried her hand at being a secretary in London without Faye's giving her another push, Kendra could not have said. But when, about four months later, Faye, back in England on another flying visit, rang her at home one night, she was to provide the push she needed.

'I've found you a flat!' Faye exclaimed without preamble.

'A flat?' Kendra echoed blankly.

'They're like gold dust in London.'

'In London?' Kendra queried, still not with her cousin.

'Of course, London,' Faye said. 'Didn't we discuss your moving to London to work the last time I was home?'

'Er—yes,' Kendra agreed, even though she was not very sure just then how the conversation had gone.

'Good,' Faye answered. 'Now...' She had then outlined how a new girl in the troupe was having qualms about leaving her younger sister behind when the troupe went abroad. Apparently, the younger sister was a quiet, introverted kind of a girl, but since she could not meet all of the rent on her salary, a flatmate would have to be found for her when her elder sister moved out. The worry was to get the right sort of person. 'I instantly thought of you,' Faye had ended. 'You and Janice should get on well together.'

It was not the fact that Faye had found her somewhere to live which had spurred Kendra on to give her notice in, but the fact, the painful fact, that Faye had obviously put her in the same quiet and introverted group as the unknown Janice.

Having given notice at her work that she would be leaving, Kendra could not have been more relieved at her parents' understanding of her plans. 'Thank goodness your mother taught you how to cook,' her father had said with a twinkle in his eye. 'At least we shan't have to worry that you'll be starving yourself.'

All in all, right from the meeting with Janice Copson, whom Kendra found nowhere near as introverted as Faye had implied, everything had gone very smoothly. In no time at all she had left Barton Avery and was housed in the London flat. In no time at all, too, she had found herself another secretarial post. Though, if she could not have said with any truth that her job at Sollis Refrigeration Limited was any more exciting that her job with the 'cruddy' solicitors, then at least the pace of work there left her with no time at all in which to brood about it.

Time had gone on, then, with her and Janice getting on famously. Kendra had seen nothing of Faye the next couple of times she had returned to England. She was in regular contact with her parents, though, so it had not taken long for the news to reach her that Faye, on a recent return to England, had paid another of her flying visits to Barton Avery, when she and her father had quarrelled most appallingly.

'It's all so silly,' Kendra's mother had commented when she had telephoned her and had spoken of the row. 'All Leslie did was to make some passing reference to the amount of make-up she wore, and Faye flew off the handle. Now they're not speaking, and Leslie's said that she'll apologise before he will.'

'Oh, dear,' Kendra had murmured, fully aware that Faye had inherited a goodly share of her father's stubbornness—even then, though, she had not expected hostilities between father and daughter to last so long.

She had thought her cousin to be overseas somewhere when some six months later she had rung to say that she was in London. To Kendra's enormous surprise, Faye had told her that she was giving up her dancing career to be married—the following day!

Faye, it seemed, wanted some member of her family to be present. 'What about Aunt Heather and Uncle Leslie?' Kendra had enquired.

'My parents won't be there,' Faye had told her. 'I know without asking that my mother won't come without my father, so I won't bother asking her.'

Kendra had been aware by the time she got to the register office the next day that she would be the sole representative of the Jephcott family when her cousin married her Greek fiancé. She'd discovered though, that Eugene Themelis had two members of his family present. As introductions were made, she had had to quickly conceal her surprise that the young, dark, curly-haired Adonis whom she had taken to be Eugene Themelis turned out to be his son Costas, from a previous marriage. Eugene Themelis himself turned out to be the mature, fortyish man who was looking at Faye adoringly. For the sake of courtesies, however, he managed to drag his eyes from his bride while introductions were made, and he shook Kendra warmly by the hand.

His son, Costas, had shaken her hand warmly too, and, with his eyes clearly expressing approval of what he saw, he had held on to her hand as he had murmured, 'You are blonde, and beautiful, like your cousin. But,' went on the young man of about the same twenty-two years as herself, as he peered into her eyes, 'where Faye's eyes are blue, yours are the most lovely green.'

Somewhat at a loss to know how to answer this young man, who quite obviously was ready to charge headlong into a flirtation, Kendra murmured quietly, 'True,' and retrieved her hand to be ready to shake hands with the third Greek present.

That was, she was ready to shake hands with the mid-thirties, grim-faced man who had been studying what was going on from his position by the window. But the 'lovely green' of her eyes left him cold, apparently, for he had seemed to have small inclination to come and take any part in the proceedings.

Most oddly then, Kendra had felt a flicker of anger ignite inside her. It was most odd, because never before could she remember taking such an instant dislike to anyone. Not that she cared whether her green eyes left him cold or whether they didn't, but he needn't look so sour-faced. It was supposed to be a joyous occasion, after all! An inbred sense of courtesy must have stirred in him, though, for as Eugene performed the introductions the man moved his long length closer.

'This is Miss Kendra Jephcott, Damon, Faye's cousin,' Eugene said in faultless English, and, requesting of Kendra formal permission to use her first name, 'Kendra, allow me to introduce my distant relative, the head of our company, and also my very good friend, Damon Niarkos.'

'How do you do,' she murmured politely as her hand was taken and enfolded in a firm clasp.

She never got to know until after the marriage ceremony if Damon Niarkos spoke the same faultless English as his distant relative. Because, as if to save him the bother of making any reply, someone came at that moment to tell them that the registrar was ready for them. Without a word, Damon Niarkos dropped her hand and turned from her.

By unspoken Greek courtesy, all conversation was in English, and it was at the wedding breakfast that Kendra had learned that Damon Niarkos spoke her tongue perfectly. Not that he said very much to her, but it was with barely a trace of accent that he addressed one or two remarks to her cousin.

Which had left Eugene to continue his courtesies as he turned to pass a remark to Kendra. 'I am so pleased you were able to join us today, and at such short notice,' he stated.

'So am I,' his son Costas chimed in enthusiastically, going on to confide, 'I'm still not sure if my father would have invited me to see him married had Damon not brought me to England this week as part of my business training.'

'Certainly I should have invited you,' his father replied, but his attention was back with his bride, and he passed his next comment to her, while Costas was quick to re-engage Kendra in conversation.

'Whether my father would have remembered he had a son working in this country had I not telephoned his hotel when I heard he was in England is, I think, doubtful. By I cannot be more pleased that I am here today,' he ended warmly.

'It's—a lovely wedding,' Kendra agreed.

'But the wedding party will soon be over,' he said, and followed up quickly, 'Perhaps I may escort you wherever you are going afterwards? Perhaps I might take you out to dine this evening?' he suggested with a beaming smile.

It was taking Kendra a second or two to adjust to the young Greek, who quite clearly did not intend to waste a moment of what might be his short time in England. But even as she prepared to tell Costas that she was busy that evening, she was aware of how, unashamedly, Damon Niarkos was now tuned into their conversation.

She tried her best to pretend she had not noticed Damon Niarkos's look of disapproval as he waited to hear her answer, and she tried to sound regretful as she told Costas, 'I'm sorry, I already have arrangements made for dinner this evening.'

'Oh,' he said, his smile dipping briefly. 'I should have realised that you must have many men wanting to take you to dinner.' His smile came out again, though, as he said, 'I shall have to ask long in advance, I can see that. Perhaps tomorrow?' he suggested. 'Perhaps I...'

Damon Niarkos bluntly cutting him off had both Kendra and Costas staring at him. 'We're returning home tomorrow,' he had said shortly.

'Tomorrow!' Costas exclaimed in some amazement. 'But I thought...'

'Tomorrow,' Damon Niarkos repeated firmly. And that, it seemed, was the end of the matter.

Kendra's first job when she returned to her flat was to ring her aunt and uncle to acquaint them with the fact that their one and only daughter had just got married. It was a job she would by far have preferred not to have, but it had transpired in a brief conversation with her cousin that she had not even let her parents know that she was being married, and Kendra could not say no when, belatedly, Faye said, 'I suppose I can't leave it for my mother to find out from any Tom, Dick or Harry. Will you tell her for me?'

'You wouldn't like to write to her?' Kendra suggested. Faye shook her head.

Weeks after the wedding Kendra was to wonder why it was, when she should by now have been on the way to forgetting Damon Niarkos and what he looked like, that out of the three Greek men who had been there that day it should be his face and thoughts of him that lingered. Her memory of what Eugene looked like, and likewise Costas, had started to grow dim, but as clear as ever in her mind was the face of the only man there who, if he had smiled, she had missed it.

Both Eugene and Costas had dark, curly hair, she remembered, but Damon's hair, although black like theirs, had only the slightest suggestion of a bend in it. His strong, unsmiling, aristocratic face was there before her again—when somebody spoke.

'Have you finished your meal?' the stewardess asked.

Kendra was immediately jerked out of her reverie. Glancing at the plastic container on the pull-down table in front of her, she saw that she had eaten everything in sight without any knowledge of what the rest of her meal had tasted of.

'It was very nice,' she thanked the stewardess, and handed the plastic packaging to her.

The flight was supposed to take around three hours or so, and as she put her watch forward to Greek time Kendra saw that there was still over an hour to go before the plane landed in Athens.

Realising that it would be two in the morning before her plane touched down, she decided to close her eyes and catch what sleep she could. Suddenly, though, the face of Damon Niarkos was swimming in front of her. Swiftly she opened her eyes again.

Drat the man, she thought crossly, but to her disgust she found that, no matter how much she did not want him there, she had only to close her eyes for him to appear. Wishing she had never conjured him up and thinking again that it was rarely, if ever, that she took such an instant dislike to anyone, she was forced to give up all thought of sleep.

Sitting open-eyed, Kendra attempted to keep Damon Niarkos from her mind by concentrating on something else. Deliberately she sent her thoughts back over what had happened on Wednesday evening after she had finished speaking with her mother on the phone.

She had been in the middle of drinking a cup of coffee, she recalled, when her telephone had rung for a second time. Again she had thought it might be Janice in need of a spot of cheering up. But once more she was proved wrong. For it was not Janice. This time it was her aunt, Faye's mother.

'Your father's just popped in to call for Leslie for their usual Wednesday hour at the George,' Heather Jephcott had begun as soon as the 'how are yous' were out of the way.

'Oh, yes?' Kendra answered pleasantly, feeling that, since her aunt had never telephoned her before, there was more to this call than that piece of information.

'Kenneth said your mother had been talking with you over the phone,' her aunt went on, by the sound of it having waited only until her husband had gone down to the village pub with his brother before she got to the phone herself. 'I've just rung your mother myself, and she tells me that you'd jump at the chance to go to Greece.' And, before her niece had worked out why her aunt was phoning her, Heather Jephcott was asking urgently, 'Will you, Kendra? Will you go to Greece for me?'

Taken more than a little aback, Kendra made giant strides to recover from her surprise, and exclaimed, 'Oh, Aunty!' in gentle sympathy, for plainly her aunt was in some distress. 'Faye's all right, I'm sure. You've nothing to worry about. Eugene thinks the world of her, and . . .'

'I'm sure he does,' her aunt interrupted, and seemed wound up as she went on, 'But he asked me to ring him back at his office, so why, if there's nothing wrong, would he go behind Faye's back to get me and her father there when he must know that things are not—right—between his wife and her parents, or she'd have insisted we were there to see her married? Oh, I know you told me at the time that they invited you and not us only because you were on the spot, and that there wasn't time for me and her father to come up from Barton Avery, but her father has never swallowed that. Which is why he's so unforgiving now,' she surged on. 'He's adamant that he won't go to Greece until Faye herself picks up the phone and invites him.' And to Kendra's horror, suddenly she was pleading, 'Oh, do go for me, Kendra! You know I can't go without Leslie!'

Yes, she knew that. As dearly as her aunt loved her daughter, she loved her husband more. Though Kendra rapidly formed the view that, in this time of Faye's being pregnant, surely it didn't matter who gave in first and buried the hatchet?

'I'm sorry, Aunt Heather,' she told her, as she quickly repressed a stray upsurge of excitement at the thought of going to Greece on her aunt's behalf. 'I can't have time off at the moment,' she added hurriedly, knowing that the whole idea was impossible. 'We're so busy at work that...'

'But weren't you telling your mother when you spoke to her the time before that you've two more weeks' holiday entitlement left which your boss had reminded you you would lose if you didn't take it before the end of December?' Heather Jephcott refused to be dissuaded from her path. 'We're already into the first week in October,' she went on swiftly, 'and surely, for him to have reminded you like he did, it must mean that your employer doesn't want you to lose your holiday.'

When her aunt got the bit between her teeth she well and truly got the bit between her teeth, Kendra thought as she put down the phone. For, somehow, she knew not how, she had agreed, *had actually agreed* to go and visit her cousin!

Not that she'd had chance to do anything else, she realised, for her aunt had been able to find an answer for every one of the arguments she had put up. To her suggestion that Faye might not want her there, but would much more likely prefer her aunt, Heather Jephcott had replied, 'And whom did she want at her wedding?' To her suggestion that maybe, since he had not invited her, Eugene might not want her in his home, her aunt had replied, 'If he cares for Faye half as much as you say he does, I'm sure he'll welcome you with open arms.'

Kendra did not know about that, but, warming to the idea of going to Greece without quite realising it, she had told her aunt that she would not dream of going unless she had a firm invitation from either her cousin or Eugene, and that in any case, she had too much work on to go before the week was out anyway.

It had been her aunt who had terminated the call. Sounding much less strained than when the call had begun, she said she would be in touch again tomorrow after she had phoned Eugene to tell him whether she and her husband would be accepting his invitation.

Kendra made her way to work on Thursday morning with one part of her not too unhappy at the thought of spending a two-week holiday in Greece with her cousin. From what she could remember of Eugene, she did not seriously think he would object to her taking her aunt's place and, as far as Faye was concerned, well, they had always got on well together. Still, no way would she go anywhere where she was not welcome.

Having decided that, busy or not, no one was *that* indispensable that they could not be spared for a fortnight, Kendra all the same delayed from asking her boss for the time off, deciding to wait until she was certain she was going. Her aunt would ring her again that night, she was sure, but in the meantime there was an added bonus. Two weeks would give her ample respite in which to know what she was going to do about Nigel Robinson. She was not in love with him and... From out of nowhere, when her thoughts were on love, a picture of Damon Niarkos had floated before her. Good grief, she'd thought in disgust, and slammed into her typewriter.

An hour later the phone on her desk had rung. It was the start of Kendra's not having a minute to breathe. 'Hello,' she said down the mouthpiece, and discovered that she was not going to have to wait until that evening to receive a call from her aunt.

'I rang Eugene, and he's absolutely delighted that you're going in our stead. So much so,' Heather Jephcott went steaming on, 'that when I told him you had to finish your working week first, he said that he'd arrange for you to fly out after work tomorrow evening.' Kendra was still catching her breath from that when her aunt said, 'He's just made a return call now—everything's settled. Your ticket is paid, and you're booked on the nine-thirty flight tomorrow evening. You'll be met at Athens airport and...' Kendra's pencil was busily jotting down times and other relevant pieces of information when her aunt, her voice growing choky, said, 'Give my girl a big hug from me, will you, love?'

'Of course I will,' Kendra replied, her own voice husky, then, realising that her aunt had gone, she put down her phone. A few seconds went by, then Kendra was going quickly across the carpet and into the office of Mr Anderson, her immediate superior. 'You know how you were saying the other day that if I didn't soon use up the rest of my holiday entitlement I was going to lose it. Well...'

Mr Anderson was not thrilled to hear that he would be without his right hand for the next two weeks. But he was fair enough to concede that Kendra had more than pulled her weight during the summer when a rush of work had coincided with staff shortages. From the moment she told him of her plans, though, it was all go. Kendra reeled from her office that night having spent a day being inundated with work which Mr Anderson did not want to leave for anyone else to do in her absence.

Having realised, too, that she would not have time to return to her flat before she went to the airport tomorrow night, she had rushed to the shops in her shortened lunch hour for bits and pieces for the fridge in case Janice came home starving.

In between sorting through her wardrobe that Thursday evening, Kendra rang Nigel to cancel their dinner-date for the following evening.

'Hello, darling!' he exclaimed softly when he recognised her voice.

Wincing at the 'darling', Kendra took a deep breath. 'About tomorrow night...' she began.

Nigel had not been pleased, but the fact that he seemed to think that he should be consulted before she made arrangements to go away on holiday told Kendra that he believed he had more rights over her than she did.

In between packing what she was to take with her, Kendra had rung her mother. 'Guess what?' she opened.

'I know, your aunt Heather told me.'

'So—I'll send you a card,' Kendra laughed, and suddenly she was feeling every bit as carefree as she felt any unattached twenty-two-year-old was entitled to feel.

She had sobered somewhat on Friday morning when she dashed off a note to leave for Janice, dashed out of the flat with all the speed her holiday luggage would allow, and dashed to her place of work.

It was all dash when she reached her office, too. For it seemed that, if she had spent a fitful night trying to stamp down growing excitement at the thought of flying to Athens, then her boss had spent a fitful night dreaming up the dozen and one things he wanted her to do before she left work that day!

Forced, if everything was to be left in apple-pie order, to work through her lunch hour, she found that any plans she'd had to go to the bank to pick up some Greek currency had to be abandoned. And when Kendra did eventually make it to Gatwick—with not a great deal of time to spare for check-in time—any thoughts she'd had of purchasing some currency at the airport went completely from her mind when suddenly she was confronted by Nigel.

'Nigel!' she gasped in surprise.

'I was a bit of a grouch when you rang last night,' he smiled. 'I didn't want you to leave the country without knowing that I can be really nice sometimes.'

'Oh, Nigel,' Kendra said helplessly, and just knew that, when he had gone very much out of his way to be there, now was not the time to tell him what last night she had realised she must tell him.

Nigel had started to recede from her mind, however, once she was seated in the departure lounge. Then her flight was being called and excitement was stirring in her again.

That same excitement was with her when the 'No Smoking' sign came on to accompany the 'Fasten Seat Belts' sign. Any minute now they would be landing in Athens.

Kendra was retrieving her luggage from the carousel when she wondered which one of the Themelis family would be meeting her. It would be lovely if it was Faye, but at this hour in the morning, not to mention her pregnant condition, Faye would be better off resting in bed.

Certain that Eugene would not let her down, for without a drachma to her name a taxi to his villa was out of the question, Kendra carried her luggage through to the arrivals area. Disappointment awaited her, though, when, no matter how she strained her eyes for sight of either Eugene's dark curly head or that of his son Costas, there was not a dark curly head to be seen.

So as not to block the way to the outside doors, she moved to one side and put down her heavy case. Suddenly, her heart began beating at an enormous rate. For, while everyone else appeared to be exiting from the building, one man, a tall man, a man without a curl to his name, but a man whose face she had never forgotten, was coming in.

Kendra swallowed hard when the night-dark eyes of Damon Niarkos sought and immediately found her. Could it be that *he* had been delegated to meet her?

She saw that the look on his face was no more friendly than it had been the last time she had seen him. There was not so much as a glimmer of a smile on his grim countenance, she observed. But he was coming over to where she stood, so he must be there to meet her—mustn't he?

CHAPTER TWO

ALL in one movement, or so it seemed to Kendra, Damon Niarkos had extended his right hand in the briefest of courteous handshakes, had taken charge of her suitcase, and was leaving her to follow him out to his car. And all, she thought crossly as she trotted after him, without a smile!

Welcome to Greece! she thought sourly when without fuss her case was stowed inside Damon Niarkos's limousine—and so was she. In next to no time they were driving away from the parking area.

A minute or so later, however, Kendra was taking herself to task. It was, after all, getting on for three in the morning, and she had to admit to feeling tired. She had no way of knowing if Damon Niarkos had snatched a couple of hours' sleep before he had driven to the airport, but it was good of him to forsake his bed to meet her.

'Thank you for coming to the airport to meet me,' she brought out politely when they had been driving along for five minutes.

He made no reply, and Kendra was again set to wonder what it was about this man that, without saying a word, he could needle her! What was it about him that, when any one of her friends could have attested to the evenness of her temperament, he should evoke an urge in her to add something short and snappy?

When another five minutes passed with Damon Niarkos not volunteering a word, Kendra stopped feeling that she'd be blowed if she would make another comment. She was trying to think more like the person she more normally was when the morose Greek was not around when she realised that it was more than high time that she asked him about her cousin.

'Faye,' she said abruptly, and paused when Damon flicked his eyes off the road to give her a brief, if arrogant, stare. 'My cousin, she's keeping well—er—in the circumstances?' she felt forced to go on.

'Quite well, I believe,' he drawled, as if to terminate the conversation.

Making allowances that he must want to get to his bed, Kendra took a steadying breath, and made another attempt to be her natural self. 'And Eugene?' she asked pleasantly.

'He, too, is well,' she was informed shortly.

Normally, his very short tone would have seen Kendra leaving her enquiries into the family's welfare right there. But, feeling sensitive that Damon might think her uncaring of Eugene's offspring from his first marriage now that her cousin was to present him with a new offspring, she thought it only fair to enquire, 'And how is Costas? Is he...?' She got no further. To her amazement, and just as though something in him had snapped, Damon Niarkos harshly cut her off.

'You'd be better employed, Miss Jephcott,' he snarled, 'in leaving the son of the house alone, to concentrate instead on the job you've been employed to come and do!'

Never more astonished, Kendra looked at him open-mouthed. But he was watching the road up ahead and appeared completely oblivious to her astonishment.

'What do y... How... Why, y...' she spluttered when she had her breath back. Then, not knowing which charge to answer first—the implication that she was there intending to set her cap at the son of the house, or the implication that Eugene had to promise to employ her before she would come and visit her cousin—Kendra suddenly managed to get one complete sentence strung together. '*Nobody's* paying me to come here!' she informed him tartly.

Damon Niarkos was singularly unimpressed. Giving her the benefit of a lofty sideways look, 'Paid your own air-fare, did you?' he enquired coolly.

Kendra bit her lip, and while wishing with all she had that she could answer yes, she no longer questioned the new-born urge to strike a male of her acquaintance. Really, Damon Niarkos just had to be the most hateful man she had ever met!

'Well, no,' she was forced to admit. 'But...' Her voice petered out. In truth, she hadn't had time to give any consideration to who had paid her fare. It had all been arranged so quickly that she'd had other priorities to think about. 'I already have a job, I'm merely taking a two-week holiday from it,' she told him stiffly, and, with a flick of her shoulder-length blonde hair, she turned and stared, unseeing, out of the side window.

Damon Niarkos had adversely affected her from the first moment she had met him, she fumed. Six months of not seeing him had not changed that.

When he pulled up outside a large villa in a well-to-do suburb of Athens, Kendra had made the heartfelt wish that she might pass her fortnight in Greece without ever having to see him again.

He had extracted her case from the boot when the most appalling thought suddenly struck her, though. And he had come alongside her on the pavement when the panicky words would not stay down. 'You don't live here too, do you?' she asked hurriedly.

'Afraid I might see too much?' he sneered.

It was open warfare! Undecided whether to kick his shins or ignore him, Kendra managed, just, to ignore him. Mutinying against him, she went with him through a rear entrance and up a floodlit garden path. Relief entered her soul when, having waited up and heard them arrive, she guessed, Eugene Themelis came out to meet them.

'Kendra!' he said warmly. Any cousin of his wife was a cousin of his, it seemed, for he kissed her soundly on both cheeks. Then he was taking her inside his large, sprawling home, asking after her flight as they went, and suggesting some refreshment before he got the maid to show her to her room.

'I had plenty to eat and drink on the plane, thank you, Eugene,' she replied as the three of them halted in a large sitting-room.

Eugene asked her if she was sure and then, good manners causing him to speak in English, he turned to Damon Niarkos and bestowed on him the same offer of some refreshment, but to Kendra's delight he added the words '... before you leave us.'

She smiled at this clear evidence that the odious creature did not dwell under Eugene's roof. With an uplifted heart she smiled on while Damon refused his relative's offer of a nightcap, which Eugene followed up with an invitation for him to dine with them that evening.

Bearing in mind that from the very beginning Damon Niarkos had taken against her, Kendra was convinced he would as soon go without his dinner as voluntarily accept an invitation to sit down at the same table as her. She therefore saw no reason to hide how much the fact that he would not dine with them that next evening pleased her. She observed how he glanced her way before he answered, and she knew without conceit that she had a very nice mouth—it had occasionally been termed beautiful. But as his dark look settled on the smiling curve of her lips, suddenly—and for the first time ever—she actually saw *him* smile.

She distrusted that silky smile, though, and she knew that she was right to distrust it when, transferring his look to Eugene, he replied, to her annoyance, 'I shall look forward to dining with you this evening.'

He was still smiling, and she was not, when he nodded a pleasant—if insincere—farewell to her, said goodnight to Eugene, and left.

Eugene turned to her when he had gone, and apologised for not coming personally to the airport. 'I had decided Costas would come to meet you,' he went on, 'and Costas was very much looking forward to being at the airport to greet you. But then he discovered that Damon had plans for him to visit one of our factories in the north on an important matter.'

'It was very good of you to arrange for Mr Niarkos to collect me from the airport,' Kendra murmured politely. She accepted that she was growing more and more tired by the minute, but she could not help but wonder why, since he was up and dressed, Eugene had not come to the airport himself.

The answer to that was explained when, telling her, 'You must call Damon by his first name—we are all family now,' Eugene showed that he was as much in love with her cousin as ever by adding, 'Damon was pleased to come for you. He knows that I will not leave my wife for so much as an hour in the dark of night.'

Kendra was thinking, how lovely, when she experienced a moment of disquiet about her cousin. 'Faye's all right, isn't she?' she asked hurriedly. 'I mean, you ringing my aunt...'

'My thought when I rang Mrs Jephcott was that it was most natural that my wife would want her mother near at this time of her carrying a child,' Eugene butted in to explain. 'But Faye will be as delighted as I am when she knows you are here.'

To Kendra's mind, that sounded every bit as if Faye had no idea she was expected! 'You mean—she doesn't...' she had started to exclaim, when a young maidservant appeared, and caused her to break off.

'This is Medea, who will attend on you,' Eugene introduced the young woman, and, taking up Kendra's suitcase, he led the way from the room, across the hall and up some stairs where, outside one of the rooms on a long landing, he handed over the case to the maid. Then he proceeded to give Medea some instructions in Greek, and then he smiled and wished Kendra a pleasant goodnight. 'Tomorrow,' he added, 'you will see for yourself how your cousin is.'

Was it her imagination, or had Eugene sounded a little worried? Kendra stepped over the threshold of a superbly appointed room and realised that she was too tired to form any accurate opinion about anything.

'Thank you, Medea,' she turned to dismiss the maid, and decided when the maid looked at her blankly that she was going to have to get Faye to teach her a few basic Greek phrases.

Feeling quite dreadful that the young maid must have been kept from her bed purely to wait on her, Kendra managed to convey by smiles and hand signs that she could cope quite well on her own.

Extracting her nightdress and toiletries from her case when Medea had left her room, Kendra felt suddenly too tired to do more than visit the adjoining bathroom for more than a cursory wash.

To lie between cool sheets was sheer bliss. But even so, even tired as she was, Kendra did not immediately fall asleep. She was not sure if it was just that it was way past her normal bedtime, but she felt over-tired, worried about Faye—when she had not felt worried about her before—and, she owned, not a little confused. By the sound of it, Eugene had told his wife nothing of his recent telephone calls to England!

Some twenty seconds later, Kendra's worries about her cousin had started to merge with thoughts of Damon Niarkos. As she had on the plane, she tried to eject him from her mind. Only this time, he refused to leave.

It was as plain as day that he had taken a dislike to her the instant they had met—though she could hardly object about that, since that instant dislike had been pretty mutual. What she did object to, though, was his comment about her leaving the son of the house alone! From what she could make of it, he seemed to think that she was there with the idea of having some sort of a flirtation with Costas! Wretched man, she fumed, wishing Damon Niarkos out of her head. And what was that bit about her concentrating on the job she'd been employed to do? And what about that crack of, 'Afraid I might see too much?'

Urgh, bother him, Kendra thought, and turned over to thump her pillow as though it might be Damon Niarkos's head. Promptly then, with his arrogant face starting to recede from her mind, she went to sleep.

Kendra had left England, where woolly sweaters were the order of the day. She awoke to find sun streaming in through her bedroom window. For perhaps about a minute she lay there basking in the excitement and joy that she had actually arrived. She was here, actually here, in Greece, in Athens, that most marvellous city!

Reaching for her watch, she sat up and looked around the room which last night she had been too tired to give more than scant attention to. Signs of luxury abounded everywhere, from the quality of the bedlinen to the deep pile of the carpet and the hand-crafted furniture.

Just as she was about to fling back the coverlet and go and run herself a bath, a tap on the door announced that she had company. Her dressing-gown was still packed away in her case, so, as a precaution against her company being someone other than her cousin, she called out, 'Come in!' from where she was.

'Kalimera, thespinis.' The maid whom Kendra had met when she had arrived came in.

'*Kalimera*, Medea,' Kendra tried tentatively. She was rewarded by a smile which suggested she had guessed right, and that *kalimera* was Greek for 'Good morning'. She was rewarded also in that the tray the maid carried bore a most welcome cup of tea.

A finger of guilt prodded Kendra that she should fall on a cup of English tea with such gladness when surely her first taste of Greece should be a cup of Greek coffee? But as Medea left, Kendra quieted her conscience. She had two whole glorious weeks in which to sample the local brew, for goodness' sake!

Glancing down to the watch in her hand, she saw that it was near enough—eleven o'clock! Startled because even though she had gone to bed late she had never meant to sleep so long, she quickly downed her tea and went to run her bath. While the bath was filling, she quickly unearthed underwear, cotton slacks and a T-shirt from her case, and headed back to the bathroom.

After the quickest of baths, and deciding to unpack her case later, Kendra left her room to go downstairs in the hope of meeting up with her cousin.

Faye was not to be found in the sitting-room, nor, she discovered, was Eugene around. Just then, though, a more mature female servant than Medea, dressed wholly in black and who, as far as Kendra could make out, was introducing herself as Sybil, made signs that she should go with her.

The room to which Sybil took her turned out to be a breakfast room, and although Kendra would much have preferred to have seen Faye than eat breakfast, Sybil, it seemed, had had her instructions. It seemed, too, that she was determined that they should be carried out to the letter, and that the visitor from England must eat some toast and marmalade before the next part of her instructions were carried out.

'Mrs Themelis?' Kendra tried, and was rewarded by a smile, but as Sybil bent to the table and extended the toast rack in her direction, Kendra saw that she had no option but to give in gracefully.

Sybil smiled again when the visitor from England sat down at the table. Again she offered the toast rack. 'Thank you,' Kendra smiled, and spread butter and marmalade on a piece of toast while Sybil poured her a cup of percolated coffee.

Ten minutes later, Kendra laid her serviette down on the table. 'Mrs Themelis?' she repeated.

Sybil was smiling again as she indicated that she accompany her. Hoping that she was not going on some wild-goose chase, Kendra kept pace with her when Sybil went along the hall and turned to go up the stairs.

Rapidly forming the opinion that Sybil had not understood her, but had thought her to mean that she had forgotten where her room was and would like some help in getting back to it, Kendra almost bleated out 'Mrs Themelis' again. But, dogging her every step of the way, she went with her to the end of the landing and, when Sybil stopped, she stopped. Sybil then knocked on the door in front of them and, smiling, she turned about and began walking away.

'Thank you, Sybil,' Kendra called quietly after her.

When no one came to open the door, Kendra knocked herself. And, when no one invited her in, she took it upon herself to open the door and peer in.

The door opened on what appeared to be a suite of rooms, and could be the private suite of Faye and Eugene, Kendra decided. She pushed the door wider open and entered what was a smaller version of the sitting-room downstairs. Deciding that she couldn't be trespassing or Sybil would never have brought her there, Kendra was nevertheless wondering if she should investigate one of the several doors leading from the room, when she noticed that one of the doors was ajar. Then, quite clearly, she heard a female voice say something rather irritable-sounding in Greek.

Kendra had no idea what was said, but, 'Faye?' she queried as she took a few paces across the carpet.

'Since I'm not getting out of this damned bed, you'd better come in,' her cousin, not at all welcoming, instructed her.

Kendra, shaking off her surprise, moved forward. 'What on earth's the matter with you?' she asked as she stepped inside the bedroom and saw her blonde-haired cousin sitting up in bed and looking a mite peevish.

'You've got eyes! Can't you see?' Faye responded, and sounded totally unlike the Faye she knew, loved and remembered.

It seemed to Kendra then that, short of turning around and catching the next plane home, there was only one way to tackle this.

Hiding her hurt that her cousin did not seem a scrap pleased to see her, Kendra drew on her years of experience of growing up with Faye—and her occasional moods. Without more ado, she went and gave her a hug and a kiss of greeting. 'The climate,' she said on standing back to look at her, 'doesn't appear to agree with you.'

Faye gave her a slightly self-ashamed look, though her tone was short as she retorted, 'Being pregnant does not agree with me!'

'You're feeling ill?' asked Kendra quickly.

'Every time I look in the mirror!' Faye replied in disgust. 'God,' she sighed, eyeing her small lump, 'I'm ugly!'

Kendra's breath caught, and suddenly she was recalling how Faye had always hated ugliness in any shape or form. It was then that she had an insight into what was troubling her.

'Oh, love,' she said softly, 'you're far from ugly!' And, sure she had heard it somewhere, she went on, 'Why, everyone knows that a woman is at her most beautiful in her fifth month of pregnancy.'

'Which means it has to be downhill all the way from now on, then!' Faye answered sourly.

Some minutes followed while Kendra sat on the side of the bed and tried to get her cousin to see herself in a better light. But Faye, who for the most part had always appeared to be supremely confident, did not want to know. Kendra next sought to find out—since it was midday and her cousin was still in bed—if there was anything she had to be careful about in these months of waiting. She discovered that, apart from the fiendishness of early-morning sickness, there was nothing else wrong with her. Nothing else, that was, other than the fact that Faye had the idea she looked perfectly hideous.

When further tentative questioning revealed that, rather than 'flaunt her shape' in public, with the exception of dinner, Faye chose to keep to her private rooms, Kendra realised that Eugene must be more than the 'little' worried which she had fleetingly thought he might be. His telephone call to Faye's mother had, quite definitely, been a cry for help! Loving Faye as he did, he must be worried to death about her!

'Sitting up here for most of the day can't be any good for the baby, can it?' Kendra suggested.

'Who the hell cares!' Faye said off-handedly.

Feeling disturbed that, by the sound of it, her cousin did not want her baby, Kendra told her, 'I care. And, more importantly, so does Eugene.' Faye continued to look singularly unaffected, and Kendra bottled down both surprise and anxiety that she had never expected to walk into anything like this, and tried another tack. 'Eugene must be more than a little concerned about you,' she hinted to her cousin.

'So he should be,' Faye replied, and to Kendra's amazement she was suddenly erupting to exclaim, 'My God, I might have married him for his money, but I'm damn well paying for it!'

Having witnessed with her own eyes that Eugene was in love with her cousin to the point of being obsessed by her, Kendra was shaken to her very foundations to hear her openly state that she had married him for his money. She surfaced from her shock, though, to realise that Faye could only be saying that she was paying for her avarice by carrying Eugene's child.

'S-surely,' she stammered, 'you didn't have to go in for a baby unless you *both* wanted one?'

Faye gave her a condescending look as though to say that she knew nothing, but did own, 'Oh, Eugene had said before we married that he'd like us to start a family as soon as I was his wife. I'd no intention of complying, of course, but...' her voice faded, but it grew strong again as she resumed tightly, 'I must have had a brainstorm or something, but I decided to give him the baby he wanted when he was upset that I wasn't a virgin when we married. Greeks are like that!' she exclaimed, and angry colour washed her pale cheeks as she went on, 'It's all right for him, of course. I don't suppose for a minute that he stayed celibate after his first wife died!'

'Well, what's done now is done,' Kendra said placatingly, and quickly sought for another subject. Though the best she could come up with was, 'Where is Eugene, by the way?'

'Regardless of the fact that it's Saturday, he's gone to his office,' Faye replied a degree peevishly.

'Well, I don't suppose anyone can make a success of a business by working a rigid five-day week,' Kendra soothed.

'The firm's gone from success to success ever since Damon became the head of it,' Faye revealed, 'so Eugene didn't have to go into the city today.' She paused and then, if reluctantly, she said fairly, 'Perhaps I shouldn't complain. He's had quite some time off recently.'

From that, Kendra guessed that Eugene's concern for his wife had been such that he had stayed home rather than go to his office. She guessed too that, a very worried man, he was taking this opportunity of her, his wife's cousin, being there to go to his office to do a little catching up.

'Er—how about Costas?' she asked. 'He works for the firm too, doesn't he?'

'Yes, but under Damon,' Faye enlightened her, going on, 'Just occasionally Eugene and Costas strike sparks off each other, so it's considered best all round if Costas does his training under Damon's wing, so to speak.'

Faye, Kendra thought, was starting to sound more chatty than mercurial, and she further encouraged her by asking, 'Does Costas have his own place, or does he live here?'

'He lives here, and we get on well,' Faye volunteered. 'He's tickled pink, too, at the idea of having a half-brother or sister.' To Kendra's relief, her voice had evened out when she added, 'He's away on some business or other which Damon said couldn't wait while he delayed to meet you at the airport.'

'It was kind of Eugene to ask Mr Niarkos to come and meet me,' Kendra commented, with some effort of will managing to push out a smile.

'Eugene wanted to come himself when Costas had to go away, but he has this idea that a pregnant woman shouldn't be left alone in the middle of the night,' Faye said, and a hard edge had come into her voice.

'It was kind of him to arrange to have me met, anyway,' Kendra restated quickly, and to her utter astonishment she found herself saying, 'And it was very good of Mr Niarkos, too.' Good grief! she thought, but she was further astonished when, her tongue intent on going its own way, it seemed, she heard herself ask, 'Do he and his wife live in Athens?'

As if she cared a row of worry beads where he lived! And she was darned sure that she didn't give a tuppenny damn whether he was married or not either. Which, she realised a moment or two later, made it most peculiar that she should actually feel something very like relief when Faye, perking up enough to smile, replied, 'The woman who catches him will have to be up very early in the morning. Half the beautiful females around here—a few with their eyes on the fatness of his wallet—are after him. So far, though, he's managed to remain a bachelor.' She half smiled once more, as she added, 'Eugene's of the opinion that, when Damon does succumb, he'll fall so hard he won't know what's hit him.'

Keeping such sweet thoughts as, let's hope it's a brick wall, to herself, Kendra quickly dragged her thoughts as far away from Damon Niarkos as possible. She had been with her cousin for some while now. Long enough, at any rate, for Faye to have got in an enquiry about her parents, had she any such intention. Kendra was aware then that, even if Faye was bursting to ask after her parents, her stiff-necked pride would prevent her from mentioning them. It was about time, she considered, that somebody did so.

'Your mother and father send their love,' she smiled.

'*And* father?' Faye queried.

Her bluff called, Kendra recognised that her cousin knew her father too well to be fooled. 'So I'm a liar,' she said.

'Nice try, anyway,' Faye replied quietly, but she went on sincerely, 'Now that you've come, and you've seen the mess I look, I'm glad you're here.'

'Oh, love,' Kendra said gently, and knew that she could talk to Faye until she was blue in the face, but Faye was just not going to believe she was anything but ugly.

Kendra stayed with her for another fifteen minutes, then started to make noises about going to do her unpacking. Faye then told her that meal times in the household were later than she was used to and that dinner would be around nine o'clock that evening. Shops and businesses for the most part closed between two and five every afternoon, apparently, and reopened from five until eight.

'Depending on the traffic, which, I might tell you, is absolutely impossible, Eugene will be home around three,' Faye added, and began murmuring something about going to have a bath and make herself as presentable as possible considering how the odds were stacked against her.

Kendra left her, knowing the futility of trying to get through to her cousin that she looked more beautiful than hideous.

With plenty to occupy her thoughts that warm afternoon, Kendra found that nothing could take away her pleasure of actually being in Greece. She unpacked, feeling that after the rush of the last couple of days it was a joy to have nothing more urgent on hand than to shake out and hang up the clothes which would see her through her holiday.

Just after three Medea came and, communicating by signs, had Kendra following her down to the dining-room. Realising that Eugene would be having his meal with Faye in their private rooms, Kendra ate as much as she required and then decided to explore the garden.

To lighten her heart she discovered not only that the garden was a delight but that over to the right, and far away from the path which she had trod on her arrival, was a fairly large swimming pool.

She promised to give herself the pleasure of trying it out at the first opportunity, and it crossed her mind to wonder how she had missed seeing the pool when she had been on this path before. On returning to her room, she did not have to wonder about it for long. Apart from being tired, she had been more intent on bottling down her anger with Damon Niarkos than on checking around to see if the swimsuit she had packed on the off-chance might be put to use.

Against all her wishes, she found Damon Niarkos extremely difficult to eject once he had entered her head. Several times, as the afternoon wore on and became evening, she was compelled to make deliberate efforts to send him from her thoughts.

She made herself think of Faye, and of how she had staggered her when she had said that she had married Eugene for his money. To hear her talk, too, it would sound as if she had no liking for her husband at all. And yet Kendra was not so sure. If Faye was as completely selfish as she made herself out to be, then by no stretch of the imagination would she have agreed to have a baby, would she? True, Faye might have garnered one or two hard edges since she had left Barton Avery, but surely she could not have changed so fundamentally from the for the most part good-natured elder cousin she had grown up knowing?

Besides... Faye went from her mind when, from nowhere, a picture of Damon Niarkos shot into Kendra's head. Suddenly, she was recalling how he had more or less accused her of having to be paid to come. She recalled his implication that, since she had come to Greece, it must be only so that she could set her cap at the son of the house. Just as vividly, too, she recalled his taunt, 'Afraid I might see too much?' And suddenly she knew unquestionably that Damon Niarkos, with his experience of marrying-minded females—a few with their eyes on the fatness of his wallet—was aware that Faye had married Eugene for his money, and thus had put her in the same class!

It was about a quarter to nine when Kendra descended the stairs and walked along the hall to the sitting-room. She had wondered if she would be the first down, but discovered as one person remained seated while two others got to their feet that everyone was there save her.

Not wanting to speak to Damon Niarkos unless she absolutely had to, she murmured a pleasant general greeting when three pairs of eyes looked her way.

'Good evening, Kendra,' Eugene smiled, and, moving towards her, asked, 'What can I get you to drink?'

'A sherry, please,' she requested, and aware—his good manners holding up—that Damon Niarkos was waiting for her to sit down before he retook his seat, she went over and took a chair next to her cousin. 'It was tipping down with rain where I was this time yesterday,' she told

Faye, glad to find that when one was stuck for a subject, the British climate never failed.

Shortly after that, the four of them went in to dinner. Because she too had been brought up properly, Kendra would have found it unthinkable that anyone else present should feel in any way uncomfortable on account of anything she said or did. She therefore took pains to hide the animosity she was feeling towards one certain party at the dinner-table. *Her* good manners, too, held up when, with every show of courtesy, that particular party enquired, 'You have recovered from the lateness of your flight, Miss Jephcott?'

'Yes, thank you, Mr Niarkos.' Her mouth smiled.

'What's this "Miss Jephcott", "Mr Niarkos"?' Eugene suddenly wanted to know. 'Please,' he said to Kendra, 'we are all family, and I'm sure Damon wishes that you use his first name. Is that not so, Damon?'

Kendra looked at Damon Niarkos, her mouth still smiling, only her eyes frosty as she waited for him to say that he wished nothing of the kind. She saw his glance go from her eyes to her mouth, and back to her eyes again, and she observed that there was a fair degree of frost in his eyes too. Though, if not a smile, there was a pleasant look to his well-shaped mouth when, 'Of course,' he lied, and added, 'Kendra.'

They adjourned to the sitting-room after dinner where, with every semblance of cordiality towards Damon, Kendra sat drinking coffee. She could not pretend to be other than relieved, though, when Eugene suddenly remembered that he had something he wanted to show Damon in his study.

'You will excuse us, Faye, Kendra?' Eugene asked charmingly. 'It will take but a moment.'

'That's a pretty dress,' Kendra remarked once the two men had gone.

'It's one of the few non-fitting dresses I possess,' Faye answered, starting to sound fed up. 'But since I don't intend going anywhere until this little lot's over, I shan't have any need whatsoever to go shopping for any of those horrendous bell-tent affairs.'

'You can't stay shut up in the house for the next four months!' Kendra protested, alarmed.

'Watch me!' Faye retorted. 'I'm sure as hell not going out on public display until this living nightmare is done!' She seemed about to add something more, something fairly acid, and then instead, she sighed. 'But I don't suppose you'll be here to "watch me", will you?' she said forlornly. 'How long *can* you stay?' she asked, to Kendra's ears sounding as though she was doing her best to cheer up.

'I've got to be back at my job two weeks on Monday,' Kendra told her, and they were both silent for a while.

Then, as if she had been mulling over what Kendra had said about having to go back because of her job, Faye trotted out idly, 'If you married for money, you wouldn't have to go to work. You could stay on here with me—indefinitely,' she added.

'And what about my husband?' Kendra laughed, not taking her a bit seriously, but pleased to have this endorsement that Faye had meant it when she had said she was glad she was there. 'Don't you think he might want me to live with him?'

'There is that, I suppose,' Faye said glumly, and all too obviously she had gone so very far into her own thoughts that she did not notice, as Kendra did, that one of the men, the taller of the two, had silently come into the room just as she advised unhappily, 'A thing to remember when you marry for money is to take darn good care that the man you've sold yourself to doesn't make you pregnant.'

Kendra had thought Damon Niarkos's glance had held a fair degree of frost before, but as Faye finished speaking, she saw that it was not merely frost which his dark eyes held, but ice! Quite clearly, he thought he had come in at the tail end of her *asking* her cousin for advice!

Feeling more dreadful than she ever had in her life, Kendra just knew as she sat wanting to shrivel up and crawl away that there was nothing she could possibly say now that would have him believe anything other than that she was out to marry money.

With her pride dented that anyone, even he, could think that of her, all she could do was to tilt her chin a fraction or two higher and thereby let him know that she cared nothing for his opinion anyway. She was very grateful, however, that a moment later Eugene joined them and Faye, perhaps recognising his not so silent footsteps, raised her head and—smiled.

Very soon afterwards, Kendra made sounds about going to bed. 'Goodnight,' she said generally as she left the room.

Only two voices had answered, she reflected as she went up the stairs. Not that she was bothered! Grief, she wasn't waiting with bated breath for Damon Niarkos to wish her goodnight!

It did not take her long to wash and to get into bed. Though when she lay down, she did not immediately go to sleep. For goodness' sake—she was sure she was not a whit bothered that he had the wrong idea about her! The whole notion was laughable.

Nevertheless, when Kendra eventually fell asleep, she was no further forward in finding out why, then, she should feel so disquieted inside.

CHAPTER THREE

KENDRA awoke early the following morning. A prickle of annoyance smote her when, before she could so much as welcome the day, thoughts of Damon Niarkos were with her. In an instant she had banished him. She was here, in Greece, and, unlike England's stormy weather, the sun was shining.

Leaping out of bed, she decided to think positively. She was under the shower when her positive thinking yielded up the fact that she was positive she did not give two hoots what Damon Niarkos thought of her anyway! Also, she was positive that his inclusion at dinner last night was a one-off, and that she positively would not see anything more of him during her stay.

Stepping out of the shower, she was in the act of rubbing herself dry when she suddenly remembered the swimming pool which she had intended asking permission to use. She had forgotten all about asking permission, though.

In the hope that maybe Eugene was an early riser and might be somewhere about downstairs, Kendra quickly collected her swimsuit. A few minutes later, with her swimsuit concealed by a towelling robe, she left her room and, quietly, lest she was the only one awake, she went down the stairs.

Eugene, however, was nowhere to be seen, but the servant Sybil was. By dint of Kendra's making swimming motions, it was no time at all before Sybil was escorting her outside and showing her where the swimming pool was. Despite being already aware of its direction, Kendra thanked her, and went to the water's edge.

In no time at all, she was in the water and enjoying the warmth of the sun in the heated pool. Blissfully and without conscience she thought of her friends back in England, all wrapped up for winter's onslaught. A stray whisper of thought about Nigel Robinson blighted her bliss, however, but in the process of doing a couple of energetic lengths she soon banished him from her mind.

Most oddly, though, when someone all at once splashed into the pool beside her, it was Damon Niarkos who occupied her thoughts. Suddenly, as she trod water and watched while a dark head neared the surface, her heart, for no reason whatsoever, began to pound at an alarming rate.

When that dark head broke the water, Kendra just could not fathom the sensation that she so unexpectedly experienced. Because, as she recognised that it was not Damon who had joined her in the water but Costas, and her heartbeats settled, she felt that the emotion which had beset her had been, ridiculously, somehow akin to disappointment!

She scorned the idea that she was in any way disappointed, and it was perhaps the rejection of that amazing notion which was responsible for her going to opposite extremes and greeting her host's son far more warmly than she might otherwise have done. For, 'Costas!' she cried, and beamed at him one of her happiest smiles.

'I knew I was right to drive through the night to get home!' he exclaimed, and, swimming close up to her, he trod water too as he caught hold of her and kissed her on both cheeks.

Kendra decided that it was quite time to back off—somehow his kisses to her cheeks did not have the same discretion which his father's had had. 'What time did you arrive?' she enquired as she paddled backwards to put some water between them.

'In time to see you testing the water with your big toe,' he replied, to her surprise.

'You haven't been to bed yet!' she exclaimed.

'I wanted to say hello to you first,' he smiled.

'Oh,' she said and, when she would have liked to swim several more lengths of the pool, it suddenly seemed churlish to turn her back on him to do so. Using a side stroke, she faced him as she told him, 'I'm getting out,' and made for the steps.

Costas had joined her by the time she had her towelling robe around her. 'You haven't taken breakfast yet?' he queried.

'Not yet,' she replied.

'Then we will breakfast together. In ten minutes?' he enquired.

Kendra thought of her long, thick hair. 'If you don't mind me sitting at the breakfast table with wet hair.'

'May I dry it for you?' he asked.

'No, you may not,' she answered primly. And when he grinned, she could not help but follow suit.

It took Kendra a little longer than ten minutes to join Costas in the breakfast-room. He stood up as she entered and, with his eyes on her as she seated herself, 'Yes, they are,' he announced, and when she stared, mystified, he shot her another smile. 'Your eyes really *are* the lovely green I remembered them,' he said.

By then, Kendra had realised that Costas was the most relentless flirt. 'How did your business go?' she asked him pleasantly, of the opinion that he needed no encouragement whatsoever.

He shrugged, smiled that she apparently was not going to flirt back, and queried, 'The business Damon sent me to do?'

'You were—er—up north, I think someone said,' she replied.

'I would much have preferred to remain here,' he smiled. 'But,' he sighed, 'though I wished to be at the airport to meet your plane, I could not refuse when Damon requested I should travel on business.'

Kendra found Costas easy to talk to, and breakfast was a pleasant affair. She ate her way through the toast and marmalade which Costas translated to Sybil was all she required, while he taught her one or two Greek words for future reference.

'Efharisto,' she tried out her Greek 'thank you' when Sybil came and replenished her coffee-cup.

'Parakalo,' the servant responded, a word that, as Kendra understood it, as well as meaning 'please' was also said to indicate, 'you're welcome'.

As the smiling Sybil went away, Kendra discovered that she too was smiling. She glanced across at Costas and saw that he also was smiling broadly. Why then she should suddenly think of Damon Niarkos, and how rarely he smiled, she could not have said. Before she could wonder about that odd fact, though, Costas's father came into the room.

Forgetful that she could not understand his tongue, his surprise at seeing his son caused Eugene to speak in Greek as he warmly greeted him. Costas's replying to him in English, though, had Eugene quickly apologising to her.

'Forgive me, Kendra, and good morning,' he said, the charm with which he said it causing her to see some of why her cousin had fallen for him.

'Good morning,' she responded, and she smiled brightly at him because she did not want him or anyone else to guess at the thoughts that had just come to her. For only then was she remembering that Faye had not married Eugene because she had fallen for him, but because of his money.

Having drifted off a little, she tuned back into the conversation to hear Costas telling his father that he had only just arrived home after hours and hours of driving.

'I'm glad that you found time to shave,' Eugene commented drily, and as Costas grinned and told him how he had quickly shaved after first taking a dip in the pool, Kendra observed the comfortable and loving relationship between father and son.

'How is Faye?' Costas asked.

'She's not well this morning,' Eugene replied, and looked so worried for a moment that Kendra started to wonder if Faye was suffering from more than morning sickness.

'May I go and see her?' she found herself cutting in to ask.

Some of Eugene's worried look left him as he smiled gently and said, 'I wish you would, Kendra. I believe my wife would welcome the company of another woman. She definitely does not like to be ill in front of me.'

'You can't blame her, *Pateras*!' Kendra started to fold her napkin as Costas explained to his father, 'It's natural that she doesn't want her new husband to see her in—er—this discomfort.'

'I blame her for nothing,' Eugene corrected his son. 'More, I blame myself that through me she has to put up with this distress.'

'I'll go and see her now,' Kendra said, rising quickly to her feet.

'Shall I see you again this morning?' asked Costas eagerly.

'You won't last the day if you don't catch up on some of your sleep,' his father slotted in.

'I shall see you at lunch, then, Kendra!' Costas called after her as she went from the room.

Thinking that if Faye was still being poorly she would not want to be bothered with answering doors, Kendra gave the briefest tap on the door of the upstairs suite, then entered the private sitting-room. When there was no sign of Faye, she crossed the carpet to the bedroom door. Again she knocked only briefly, then opened the door and popped her head round.

'Only me,' she said on observing her cousin sitting up in bed looking ashen-faced and exhausted. 'Can I come in?' Faye nodded. 'How are you feeling?' Kendra asked gently as she approached the bed.

'Like death,' Faye replied.

'Is it morning sickness?'

'According to the doctor—whom Eugene drags out of bed at least once a week—it is.'

'Does it happen *every* morning?' Kendra asked, her heart going out to her.

'Most mornings,' Faye replied, and looked very sorry for herself. 'Whoever called it morning sickness wants his head examining—I sometimes feel just as rotten as this in the evening. I've a feeling,' she sighed, 'that this is going to be one of those days.'

'Oh, poor love,' Kendra crooned.

'Don't sympathise with me or I'll start to howl,' Faye said in a fractured kind of a voice. 'I look enough of a wreck now, without having red eyes in the bargain.'

'Costas is home!' Kendra abruptly changed tack to tell her cheerfully.

She was rewarded by a smile as Faye, only two years older than Costas in years, said sincerely, 'He's a super kid. You'd think he might be a shade miffed about his father marrying again, but not a bit of it. All he wants is that his father should be happy.'

Smiling too, Kendra told her how Costas had driven 'through the night', and gave her view that he had probably taken himself off to bed for a few hours.

In all, she spent most of the morning with Faye. At one time, when Faye said she was starting to feel better, Kendra made the suggestion that perhaps she'd feel better still if she got bathed and dressed and came and sat outside in the garden for a little while. Her suggestion did not meet with favour, and Faye was at her most antagonistic when she told her that she could keep such ideas to herself.

Shortly afterwards, she apologised. 'I'm sorry,' she said contritely. 'I didn't mean to snap your head off. It's just that... Oh, hell, I'm not fit to be seen.'

Unable to convince her otherwise, Kendra stayed talking to her, but got up to leave when Eugene arrived to see his wife.

'Don't go!' Faye said abruptly when she saw what she was about. And, excusing that it looked as though she did not want to be left alone with her husband, 'I'm enjoying having you here.'

Kendra saw the way Eugene, his thought only for Faye apparently, looked pleased to hear her say that she was enjoying something. He stayed only to satisfy himself that she was looking better, then he asked to be excused, and left them to it. Kendra resumed her seat.

It was getting on for one when Faye decided that she would take a bath. 'I'd better do something about making myself presentable for lunch,' she told Kendra. 'Eugene will most likely have lunch with me, and if Costas surfaces he'll keep you company downstairs.'

'Do you need any help?' Kendra thought she had better volunteer as she assisted her out of bed.

'I've been bathing myself for years now, duckie,' Faye said drily, and as Kendra burst out laughing at this glimpse of the Faye she knew better than the Faye she had discovered in Greece, Faye could not resist a grin of her own.

Kendra's companion at lunch was Costas. A Costas in fine form by the sound of it as, tucking into his first course, he enquired, 'And what would you like to do this afternoon?'

'I'm—pardon?' Kendra queried.

'Where shall we go?' he asked. 'Where shall I take you?'

'Oh,' Kendra murmured, and as she caught on she quite liked the idea of going out.

'You've no need to worry about Faye,' he told her earnestly, as if sensing that she was demurring on account of her cousin. 'My father, I promise you, will, as he does each Sunday, spend the afternoon with her. Would you,' he beamed, 'wish to be a—a strawberry?'

'A straw...' Suddenly Kendra was smiling too. She had no desire at all to come between husband and wife, and the idea of going out was taking on greater appeal by the second. But, because she had recognised Costas for the flirt he undoubtedly was, she did not rush to snatch at his offer, but told him, 'I've no wish whatsoever to be a—gooseberry.'

'Gooseberry,' he repeated to himself, and, having noted the correction, he stuck to his original questioning as he asked, 'Where would you like to go this afternoon?'

Kendra had seen pictures of the Parthenon countless times, and had always wanted to visit it. Suddenly, it seemed unthinkable that she should return to England without having done so.

'Is it far from here to the Acropolis?' she asked, having read enough to know that the Acropolis stood on its rock, and that the crown of the Acropolis was the Parthenon.

'Subject to the traffic's not being as murderous as it usually is in Athens, I think I could get you there in half an hour,' Costas said, delighted that she had agreed to his taking her out.

'It's that near to where we are?' she asked in some surprise.

'Oh, yes,' Costas replied, but he was grinning as he added, 'Although I do happen to have a very fast car.'

From that, Kendra gathered that, whether speed restrictions operated in Athens or not, Costas was a law unto himself when he was behind a steering wheel.

Costas was all for them going straight away once lunch was over, but Kendra insisted that she must go upstairs to change first. 'But you look beautiful just as you are!' he exclaimed.

'I'll see you in fifteen minutes,' she told him.

In her room she exchanged her dress for a pair of cotton trousers and a T-shirt. Bearing in mind, too, that some of the centuries-old ruins which she might be tramping over deserved something better than the harsh heels of the court shoes she had worn at lunch, she quickly found a pair of soft-soled flat shoes to put on.

This time, she was under the time she had stated when she went tripping lightly down the stairs. With eager anticipation starting to soar at what she would shortly see, she went blithely into the sitting-room and began to address the back of the man who stood there.

'How's that for...' She stopped dead. For the man who turned round at the sound of her voice was taller than Costas, and the fact that his hair was not remotely as curly as it should have been set her heart drumming in the most peculiar of fashions.

'How's that for—what?' Damon Niarkos queried coolly, as he fixed his dark gaze on her wide green-eyed expression.

'For—timing,' she replied, and got herself more together to add, 'I thought you were Costas.' When he continued to stare at her, she explained, 'He finished the job you sent him on, and he's back home.'

'Correction,' Damon replied. 'He has neither completed the job, nor is he at home.'

'He's—not at home?' Kendra queried.

'Costas has just realised that he had forgotten to give the findings of the job he was on to the computer department,' Damon told her, as though he'd had nothing to do with prodding Costas's memory about his omission. 'The computer terminals get so very busy during the week,' he unbent sufficiently to inform her, 'that Costas, knowing we have a few operators in today, thought he had better delay no further.'

'So—he's—gone to your offices to...' Her voice tailed off as Damon nodded. 'I see,' she said slowly, and as her eager anticipation of the sights she would see that afternoon started to recede, 'He'll be away some time, I expect?' she questioned.

'It's not a job anyone can complete in five minutes,' Damon replied.

'Of course not,' she murmured, and, Damon Niarkos being more a member of this Greek family than he would ever be a friend of hers, she turned and was half-way from the room when his voice suddenly caused her to halt.

'Apparently, Costas was most anxious that you should not miss going to the Acropolis,' he drawled.

'I can go another day,' she told him.

'There's no need,' he remarked, and to her utter astonishment, he actually added, 'I'll take you.'

Grief! Kendra thought, but she wasn't having any autocrat taking her anywhere out of a sense of duty. 'Oh, there's no need for *that*,' she bounced back at him, and cared not a jot that he frowned when he could see she could be a trifle autocratic herself on occasion.

She was, therefore, even more astonished when he would not take no for an answer. 'I must insist,' he told her coldly. 'Costas has promised to take you, but because of the work I want done he cannot. I must, therefore, honour his contract for him.'

'You don't have to do anything of the kind!' Kendra was quick to tell him. But she could see, when Damon had nothing further to add, that she was up against Greek honour here. While she was quite happy to offend Damon Niarkos, though, *and* his Greek honour too, she suddenly realised that in doing so she could very easily be at risk offending the whole of his family for all she knew—no matter how distantly related. The last person she would wish to offend was Eugene, so she therefore, reluctantly, saw that she had better climb down. 'I shouldn't like to put you to any trouble, Mr Niarkos,' she said stiffly, and did not get to hear him state whether it would be a trouble to him or not, because just then Eugene came into the sitting-room.

'Kendra and I are just off sightseeing,' Damon told him, as if there was no question but that it was all settled.

'You don't mind, do you?' Kendra asked, uncertain, now that she again had the chance to visit the Acropolis, if she did want him to object.

'Of course I don't mind,' Eugene smiled. 'I want you to enjoy yourself. I myself will sit quietly with my wife,' he added, and Kendra was perceptive enough to see that, plainly very much in love with his wife, he had only torn himself away from her side because he was her cousin's host, and good manners decreed he should check that she was not being neglected. At that moment Kendra knew she would have agreed to go out with the devil himself rather than keep Eugene away from his Faye for another minute.

Damon Niarkos, though, to her immense surprise, turned out to be nothing like the devil she would happily have believed him an hour ago! Without fuss or bother she was soon ensconced in his car, and they were soon driving through the wide, tree-lined streets of the Athens suburbs. Less than an hour later, Kendra was standing awestruck, looking at the citadel of Athens.

With Damon's hand at her elbow she climbed up steps and walked over wooden staging and, with her heart pounding, she gazed at—the Parthenon.

'It's—unforgettable,' she said huskily, her breath caught in wonder when, wanting to share her experience with someone, she turned to the tall man by her side.

'You seem—taken with it,' Damon commented drily as he looked down into her shining eyes. And, just as she was about to look away, a smile began to curve his lips.

It was the first genuine smile she had seen on him, and suddenly her heart was beating faster. Because it was a quiet smile, a kind smile, a smile of sharing, and without questioning why Kendra just knew that she was glad that she was here on the Acropolis with him, and not Costas.

Her heartbeats steadied as she looked away from him. And her senses, her pleasure, were once more caught up in delight as she gazed and just gazed at the fifth-century BC Doric columns of the Parthenon. For an age she looked her fill, walked on a little, and stopped to look some more. With Damon still by her side, she walked over the site, but again came back to look some more at the Parthenon.

The next time that the 'wanting to share' feeling came over her, Kendra looked up at Damon only to find that he was looking directly at her and nowhere else! 'It's—terrific,' she whispered huskily.

'If seeing the temple of the goddess Athena can make you look so enchanted,' he murmured softly, 'then what can I do, Miss Kendra Jephcott, but take you to see Delphi?'

Again her breath seemed trapped in her throat. Delphi, she was sure, was miles and miles away! Was Damon saying that one day during her stay he would put himself out to take her there?

An emotion which she could not put a name to suddenly caught her, and all at once she felt totally vulnerable. She was aware by then that her face must be pretty expressive—or Damon's senses sharp—for him to have picked up how enchanted she felt, and she turned from him.

She had her back to the Parthenon and was studying the Erectheum opposite, with its porch of caryatids, when, 'I'm reliably informed,' Damon said suddenly in her ear, 'that the olive tree you can see growing on the left is the self-same olive tree which Athena caused to appear during her argument with Poseidon.'

Kendra looked at him then, and as she perceived what just *had* to be a teasing light in his eyes—and against all she would have thought to the contrary—she all at once felt in complete harmony with him.

Whether Damon felt that same harmony with her she had no way of knowing, but as she sat beside him on the return journey, she instinctively felt that the old animosity between them was gone for ever.

Which was perhaps why, as they drove past a bank and she recalled that she did not have a scrap of Greek currency to her name, she should have relaxed sufficiently to exclaim, without thinking first, 'Oh, a bank, I must get to a bank as soon as possible!'

'You have some urgent business requiring attention?' Damon asked, extracting his vehicle from a sudden tangle of traffic without turning a hair.

'I've an urgent need of some drachmas,' she told him easily, again, quite without thinking, as she added, 'I left England in such a rush, I didn't have time to get to my bank.'

'We cannot have that,' Damon said evenly, but went on to make her squirm with embarrassment when, reaching for his wallet while keeping one hand on the steering wheel, he said, 'Allow me to lend you...'

'Certainly not!' Kendra cut him off sharply, warm colour suffusing her face as she realised that he must think she had been fishing for him to give her some money. She caught his glance on her at her sharp tone, and any harmony she had felt between them was fractured to smithereens. 'I was not asking for a *loan*!' she went on tartly, and as it came back to her how Damon Niarkos believed she was there in his country to feather her nest, she became so wound up that words were rushing from her with her being only half aware of what she was saying. 'I was merely stating that, since everything conspired against me, what with me being too busy at my office to get to the bank, and what with Nigel appearing unexpectedly at the airport to see me off, when I would have got some...'

'Nigel?' Damon Niarkos cut in to break her flow.

'Yes, Nigel,' she said irritably. 'He's...' Suddenly she stopped, and was not quite sure how to explain her relationship with Nigel. 'He's—a friend,' she said, and left it like that.

'You mean—he's your lover?' Damon Niarkos seemed to have no problems in deciding what Nigel Robinson was to her.

Kendra meant nothing of the kind, but as far as she was concerned, Damon Niarkos could think what he liked. Without answering, she turned her head and looked out of the side window.

In stony silence they completed the rest of the journey. At her hosts' home Damon, as she had expected he would, got out of the car and went in with her. His good manners, she had realised, would see him going in to have a brief word with Eugene before he went on his way.

Together they crossed the hall but, since she had no intention of going into the sitting-room with him, when they neared the foot of the stairs Kendra remembered her own good manners, and halted.

'Thank you for your—kindness to me this afternoon,' she said, primly and like the well-brought-up person she was. Damon had halted too, and he was surveying her with, to her mind, a fairly grim expression when suddenly she remembered how he had looked at her up at the Acropolis. There had even been a teasing light in his eyes at one time, she recalled, and suddenly, perhaps because that whole wonderful experience was so recent, she found herself going on—and it had nothing at all to do with good manners, 'I thought the Parthenon, the Acropolis, absolutely magnificent.'

Only as the words left her did it come to her that, in the face of his unyielding expression, she had just made an idiot of herself. Abruptly she turned, and was about to go up the stairs when suddenly Damon's hand was on her wrist and he was turning her to face him.

Her heart missed a beat when he stared solemnly down into her large green eyes. Then, in a voice that was a whole lot warmer than it had been, he suddenly said softly, 'The pleasure, Kendra, was mine.' Then he let go of her wrist.

Kendra smiled, because she could not help it, and a second later she had turned about and, uncertain whether Damon had moved or if he was still watching her, she went on up the stairs. At the top she did not look round, but went on along the landing. The moment she was sure that she could not be observed, however, her smile broadened. Suddenly, all was right with her world.

Without knowing it, she still had a trace of a smile on her face as she opened her bedroom door. A sound further along the landing, though, caused her to look to where her cousin had just come to the outside door of her suite.

Faye's harsh-sounding, 'What's the secret smile about?' was sufficient to make Kendra swiftly straighten her features.

'Still feeling below par?' she asked gently as she went over to where her cousin stood.

But Faye was in a spleenish mood, and did not want anyone's sympathy. 'Where have you been all afternoon?' she asked, sounding jealous that Kendra had been out while she had been stuck indoors.

'Damon Niarkos called. He took me to see the Acropolis,' Kendra told her, and would have gone on to tell her how marvellous she had found it all when, to her astonishment, Faye rounded on her.

'My God!' she snorted. 'You're not wasting any time!'

'What are you talking about?'

'Don't tell me you don't know.'

'Know what?' Kendra asked.

Faye shrugged her shoulders expressively, and enlightened her, 'Eugene may be loaded, but when we get to talking about the big money, and I mean really big, then Eugene just isn't in Damon's class.'

'So?' questioned Kendra, having taken on board the fact that Damon Niarkos was probably a millionaire many times over but, for all Faye's enlightening of her, still feeling somewhat in the dark. Until suddenly all this talk of money triggered off a reminder of Faye's telling her how she had married for money. 'Good grief, Faye!' she exclaimed, startled, her cousin's accusations starting to take on some meaning. 'Surely you're not suggesting that I'm out to ensnare Damon Niarkos for his money?'

'It won't do you a scrap of good if you are,' Faye retorted. 'According to Eugene, Damon can spot a woman with drachma signs in her eyes from a mile off, and is adept at taking evasive action. And, whether you've realised it or not, I've realised that Damon must have come into the *saloni* last night just as we were discussing your selling yourself in marriage for money.' And while Kendra stood gasping, especially since it had been Faye who had been doing the talking and not her, Faye went on, 'I'm afraid, cousin dear, that you've rather tipped your hand in advance.' With that, she disappeared back inside her suite of rooms.

Kendra reeled back to her own room and went to sit on the edge of her bed. She was utterly appalled that Damon might think she was remotely interested in him for his money or for anything else. She had thought him of the opinion that she was taking advantage of being there to set her cap at Costas. But—could it be, could it really be, that he thought she was taking advantage of being there, to set her cap—at him?

Kendra remembered how, only minutes ago, she had smiled at him. How, in the interests of showing him that the British were every bit as well-mannered as the Greeks, she had almost fawned over him in her thanks for the afternoon.

Well, perhaps 'fawned' was a bit of an exaggeration, she qualified a moment later. But, as what Faye had just said hit her again, Kendra grew very determined about one thing. There would be no fawning in future. In future, she was going to be very much cooler to one Mr Damon As-wealthy-as-Croesus Niarkos!

CHAPTER FOUR

SO MUCH for my determination to show Damon Niarkos a cool front, Kendra thought as she got into bed on Monday night. A whole day had passed since that trip to the Acropolis, and she had not caught so much as a glimpse of him!

Perhaps that was the reason she was feeling so out of sorts just at the moment. Not because she wanted to see him, of course, but because by not calling at the villa again he had taken away her chance of showing him that she was not the tiniest bit interested in either him or his wallet.

Kendra took her mind off Damon Niarkos, and, realising that things in general were pretty dull just now, she attempted to discover why she should consider that she was going through a dull patch. Costas was still flirtatious, but he seemed to have adjusted a little to her being there. Although she could not in any way put the blame on him for her present dull-seeming existence.

Eugene was the same as he always was, courteous and charming. Her thoughts drifted as she thought how, in the short while she had been there, she had witnessed how much Faye was the pivot of Eugene's universe. He little short of idolised her. Countless were the times his eyes would go to Faye, and would stay on her, love there in his eyes for all to see. Only Faye apparently could not see how much Eugene seemed, not only obsessed by her, but possessed by her too.

But Faye, although it was clear that she had a tremendous respect for her husband, was still unhappily convinced that she looked a sight, and appeared unconcerned whether her husband loved her or not. At dinner this evening, though, Kendra would have sworn that Faye had looked at Eugene with a special look in her eyes.

Kendra sighed as, restlessly, she turned over in her bed. Faye had been at her most contrite when this morning she had gone to sit with her for a while. 'I was a rotten bitch to you yesterday,' she had said as soon as Kendra had sat down. 'It's a wonder to me that you've bothered to come and see me this morning.'

'Oh, you're not bad all the time,' Kendra teased, to cover how Faye's remarks had hurt her.

'I shouldn't have said what I did.' Faye refused to feel any better until she had made a full apology. 'I shouldn't have accused you of not wasting any time with Damon, when I know you just aren't interested in any man's pocket.'

'You're feeling better this morning, obviously,' Kendra said cheerfully.

'If there's any fairness in the world, I was down enough yesterday for me to have earned a brighter day today,' Faye admitted. 'Are you going to forgive me?'

'Are you going to come out in the garden with me for a little while?' Kendra countered.

'I should be *that* sorry?' Faye answered, but although she stayed in a sunnier mood for the rest of the day, no amount of teasing or cajoling would get her out of the house.

When Kendra finally fell asleep, it was on the thought that if Faye was appearing sunnier, then the same could not be said of herself. Kendra owned that she was feeling decidedly glum.

When she awoke on Tuesday morning, the answer to why she should feel so dejected when she was in such a marvellous foreign country awoke with her. That was it! Here she was, in a foreign country, on the fourth day of her holiday and so far, apart from that trip to the Acropolis with Damon on Sunday, she had not poked her nose outside!

So OK, she mused as she showered and then dressed, Eugene had paid her fare, and it couldn't be really termed a holiday-type holiday since Eugene had wanted her there, or preferably her aunt, because he was concerned about Faye. But, since she wasn't in England and at her desk, then surely she could consider it a holiday of sorts, a holiday where she and Faye might have gone on a few outings together.

That morning followed the same pattern as the last three mornings, in that Kendra went downstairs and had breakfast with Costas, while Eugene had breakfast with his wife.

'Were it not for the cruelty of my father sending me out to work,' Costas joked as he grabbed up his briefcase prior to rushing off, 'then I could stay with you all day.'

'We'll have to report him to the National Society for the Prevention of Cruelty to Children,' Kendra laughed, and was briefly cheered when Costas grinned and left her to, as he had said the previous day, 'make for the hell of the Athens traffic'.

Kendra passed Eugene coming down as she went back up the stairs. 'Good morning, Kendra,' he bade her, but to her mind he seemed to be mentally on another planet.

'*Kalimera,* Eugene,' she greeted him, but although he smiled as he passed by, she had an idea that her greeting in his own tongue had hardly registered.

Not surprised that he seemed a worried man, she stopped off at her room to do a quick tidy round, but it was in her mind to try and do something other than sit in Faye's bedroom with her for the whole of the morning. She hadn't been to the bank yet, for goodness' sake, let alone bought any postcards to send home!

Knowing that buying picture postcards was out of the question until she *had* been to the bank, Kendra went from her room to see Faye. She practised a few tactful phrases for trying to get her cousin to go to the bank with her when, crossing through the private sitting-room, she tapped on the bedroom door and entered. But seeing Faye dabbing at her eyes with a handkerchief sent any rehearsed phrases completely from her.

'Oh, love!' she exclaimed, going quickly over to the bed. 'Aren't you well?'

'I've had a row with Eugene,' Faye choked, and she turned her face away as she tried to get herself under control.

'Oh, dear,' Kendra sighed, and recalled on that instant how worried Eugene had seemed when they had passed on the stairs. Now that she knew he and Faye had quarrelled, however, Kendra realised that, this time, he had been more upset than worried. But she had no wish to pry into what the row between husband and wife had been about and, feeling a little awkward, all she could think to say was a soothing, 'Never mind, I'm sure you'll both be feeling better by lunch time.'

'You must have been listening at the keyhole,' Faye said with a shaky attempt at a smile. 'That was what the row was about.'

'About you feeling better by lunch time?' Kendra queried, suddenly forgetful that she had no intention to pry.

'About Eugene *telling me* I'd feel better then,' Faye replied, starting to look angry as she relived the conversation. 'He's no idea how I feel, so where does he get off, telling me how I'll feel?'

'Have you tried telling him how you feel?' Kendra asked gently.

'I don't see it as my role in life to bore him out of his skull on the subject of the mess I feel!'

'You're not a m...'

'I know I am,' Faye cut her off, and went on to reveal how Eugene had that morning begun by complimenting her that she seemed much improved since her cousin had come to stay. 'Then,' she went on heatedly, 'having cunningly got my agreement that yes, I did feel much cheered to have you around, he had the nerve to tell me that I'll be feeling better still by lunch time, and that, as you were my guest as well as his, it would be only your due courtesy if both he and *I* joined you and Costas for lunch.'

Kendra was not certain if Faye was blaming Eugene for his suggestion, or for the sneaky way he had got her to admit that she was feeling more cheered to have her around. But, not at all happy that she now appeared to be a bone of contention between the two of them, all Kendra felt she could say without upsetting Faye further was another, 'Oh dear.'

Again she spent the morning closeted with Faye in her room. It had never been on to get her to go out shopping with her anyway, Kendra realised, as one o'clock neared and she left Faye to take her bath.

Costas, who Kendra suspected was something of a madcap driver, arrived home half an hour before his father. '*Yassou,* Kendra!' he greeted her, his smile ever-present on his good-looking face. 'You've spent an enjoyable morning?'

'Yes,' she replied, and when lunch was announced she went with him to the dining-room where she wondered if they should wait awhile just in case Faye and Eugene joined them.

'Something wrong?' Costas enquired, taking on his father's role when he noticed that she was delaying making a start on the soup that had been placed in front of her.

'No, nothing,' she smiled, and, her napkin on her lap, she picked up her soup spoon.

Faye and Eugene did not join them for lunch, and while Costas saw nothing out of the way in this, Kendra hoped that they were not having another row over her being the guest of both of them, or over Faye's stubbornness to leave the suite until evening time.

Costas was a chatty meal-time companion and left her with little space for her own thoughts. But when, after the meal, he suggested that, as she had the day before, she came and occupied a sun lounger next to his beside the pool, Kendra shook her head. Somehow, she felt too restless to lie soaking up the last of the summer's rays.

'I think I'll go for a bit of a walk,' she told Costas when he seemed to want to know what he had done that she would not spend her siesta hour with him.

'Walk!' he exclaimed, just as though the very idea had sent a shudder along his spine. 'I have my car if...' he started to say, but Kendra cut him off.

'Walking off one's lunch is an old English custom,' she told him with a smile.

'It needs two—this walking?' Costa asked humorously.

'Have your nap,' she laughed.

Exiting from the rear entrance, Kendra was soon stepping out over the pavements. While keeping account of her whereabouts so that she did not get lost, Kendra walked through wide, tree-lined avenues, and again experienced a feeling of restlessness.

Pausing in her stride, she made a land marker of a red-roofed, shutters-closed villa where a veritable mass of vegetation cascaded down from plant-pots on the balconies. Having noted the villa for her return journey, she crossed the road and walked on, letting her thoughts leap and settle where they would.

It was not long before she was again recalling how upset Faye had been that morning. Poor Faye, she could not help thinking, she was going through a very miserable time just now. She... Suddenly, with her thoughts still on her cousin, it all at once struck Kendra that, for a woman who had married for money, and not for love, Faye had been much more upset over her row with her husband than she would have expected.

Eugene had been upset, too, of course, but he was absolutely besotted with Faye, so the fact that he should be upset that they had argued was more natural, surely?

Kendra was thinking of love when she decided to return to the villa. She turned to go back the way she had come when her thoughts came to a sudden and abrupt halt. For, just as her thoughts had flitted to wonder what type of man she herself might ultimately fall in love with, so, crazily, idiotically, the face of Damon Niarkos chose that moment to swim in front of her.

'Good lord!' she muttered, staggered, and was even more staggered when at that precise moment a car she was familiar with, since she had driven in it several times, drew up.

Out of politeness, she stopped when, just as though thinking of him had dreamed him up, Damon Niarkos stepped out of his car. She almost smiled at him. Then she was glad that she had not done so, for his expression was unsmiling and his manner brusque when, with a lift of his aristocratic head, he enquired, 'Are you lost and in need of a lift back to Eugene's villa?'

Only then did Kendra remember that this was the man to whom she was going to be very much cooler the next time she saw him. 'I'm not lost,' she told him aloofly, and hated the fact that he had got in first with the cool treatment. Realising that in the time since she had last seen him he must have decided that she *had* been setting her cap at him on Sunday, pride added a few degrees of stiffness to her voice as she tacked on, 'Neither do I require a lift, thank you.'

Kendra could not say that she was surprised when, her arrogance not going down well, apparently, Damon did not offer a second time. Without another word, he got back into his car and drove off.

Wretched man, she fumed, remembering that the last time she had parted from him his voice had been warm and she had smiled at him. She recommenced walking and, watching his car until it had disappeared from sight, she vowed angrily that she was going to be as sparing with her smiles as he was in future.

She was back at her cousin's home before it came to her to wonder why she should be so het up about him. For goodness' sake, the man meant nothing to her! Why, it would not bother her if she never saw him again.

Bothered or not, Kendra discovered that the one good thing about having something else to think about was that her fears about being a bone of contention between Faye and Eugene had been put into perspective.

By the time she was sitting down at dinner that night, Kendra had realised that Eugene, in his concern for his wife, had only used her as a tool with which to try and get Faye to spend more time out of their suite.

Happy to realise that she was not really a bone of contention between them, Kendra took her place at the dinner-table and had space to mentally reiterate that she was doubly certain it would not bother her if she never saw Damon again.

Involuntarily, though, as if pulled by a magnet, her eyes went to the place where he had sat when he had dined with them on Saturday, and suddenly, as a feeling of restlessness yet again visited her, she was launching headlong into speech.

'I like your hair—that's a new style, isn't it?' she asked her cousin.

'It is, actually,' Faye acknowledged.

'It suits you very well, my dear,' Eugene told her, and while Faye looked pleased at the compliment, and Kendra gathered that they had patched up their quarrel, Costas was attracting her attention.

'I have been thinking, Kendra, that, since you like walking so well, perhaps you might like me to take you to Delphi tomorrow.'

Instantly her thoughts went to Damon, but before she could make any sort of a reply Eugene was teasing his son, 'You intend to walk to Delphi?'

Costas grinned. 'I was speaking of the walking involved when we get there,' he replied. 'Although,' he corrected after a moment, 'maybe climbing would be more appropriate.'

'You do not intend going to your office tomorrow?' his father asked him, a shade severely, Kendra thought.

'Oh, I must go in the morning, but Damon has kept me working so hard just lately that I'm sure he cannot object if I leave my office around one o'clock. Especially,' he put in, 'since I worked all through last weekend.' Turning from his father, he again asked, 'Would you like to go to Delphi, Kendra? We can be there in two hours, and...'

'Two hours!' Eugene exclaimed.

'Well, maybe three,' Costas grinned and, turning again to Kendra, he waited for her reply.

When she thought about it, Kendra realised that yes, she would love to go to Delphi, the place which ancient Greeks believed to be the centre of the world. Again thoughts of Damon Niarkos came to her, but from his recent brusque manner with her she had a very sharp impression that if he'd ever had any intention of taking her to Delphi himself, he had rapidly gone off the idea. Not that she would have gone with him anyway.

'I'd love to go,' she smiled at Costas. He was still grinning his pleasure at her answer when, bearing in mind the spleenish mood Faye had been in the last time she had gone sightseeing, Kendra said a general, 'If that's all right with everyone?'

'Of course. You must have some enjoyment while you are with us,' Eugene told her warmly. 'Is that not so, Faye?' he asked his wife gently.

'Of course,' she echoed, and her smile was genuine as she told Kendra, 'You'll come and say hello to me in the morning, though, as usual?'

It was Kendra's turn to say, 'Of course.'

She had a lot to fill her mind in bed that night. Faye had been in a cheerful mood, which had caused Eugene to look cheerful too, and for herself, apart from the marvellous outing she had to look forward to, the gods were being kind. For surely, when mentioning to Damon tomorrow that he would be leaving his office early, Costas would tell him that the rest of his day was being spent in taking her to Delphi.

Maybe it should not please her so, she mused, as she settled down to sleep, but she would rather have Damon Niarkos thinking that she was setting her cap at Costas than at him. And what woman, having been treated the way she had by Damon Niarkos, could help but be glad at the thought that he would soon know she was not holding her breath waiting for him to follow up his intimation that he'd take her on this particular outing.

Costas arrived home around noon the following day. But any cheering thought she had that through Costas she had metaphorically thumbed her nose at Damon Niarkos disappeared when, as they drove along, she took her gaze away from a man at the roadside selling bananas, and murmured casually, 'I hope you didn't have any trouble getting the time off today. I mean,' she continued, as Costas glanced her way, 'I hope that Damon hadn't something else he wanted you to do.'

'Oh, Damon wouldn't want me to ask him for every hour I want off,' Costas told her light-heartedly. 'But,' he went on, 'since Damon had business last evening which kept him away from Athens overnight, I've not been able to see him today.'

'Oh,' Kendra smiled, and left it there.

Shortly after that they left the toll road and stopped at a small taverna for something to eat. 'Are you sure?' Costas enquired when she said that she fancied moussaka.

'I haven't had any yet,' she told him. 'How can I go home without having tried it?'

They did not linger over their meal, and soon afterwards they were on their way again, with Costas sending the sports car speeding over the National Highway Number One. Only when he slowed down was Kendra able to appreciate where white and pink oleanders interspersed with pyracanthas to line their route, and where, backing the white, pink and orange colours, were olive trees, pistachio trees, and tall cypresses.

Then they were driving through plains which seemed surrounded in mountains. And then, quite breathtakingly, they were at Delphi. It was then that Kendra appreciated what Costas had meant when he had corrected his reference to the walking they would do when they got to Delphi, and had said that maybe climbing would be more appropriate, for Delphi was built on the side of a mountain, and the only way to see the various ruins was to climb up.

Strangely, though, when there was much to see and marvel at, for Kendra something was missing that afternoon. 'It's quite splendid,' she told Costas as she stood studying the remains of the temple of Apollo, the chief god at Delphi. 'Quite staggering,' she murmured as they climbed higher to reach the semi-circular open-air theatre. And, when they had taken the steep path up to the open-air stadium which was said to accommodate seven thousand spectators, she was quite open-mouthed. But the whole of the while, something was taking the edge off her enjoyment. Somehow, she was not getting the same thrill which had been there when she had been at the Acropolis with Damon.

'You're going to want to have a look at the museum of Delphi too, aren't you, Kendra?' Costas queried as they made their way down from the stadium.

'Can we?' she asked, and saw more to wonder at when, the museum within walking distance, she looked at the various statues and artefacts on display.

Her head was still full of the Sphinx of the Naxians which in the sixth century BC had stood on a tall column in the temple of Apollo, when, as they were leaving the museum, Costas declared that he could do with some refreshment.

'You enjoyed that?' he enquired when, descending to the road below, they saw a mobile refreshment bar and walked over to it.

'Very much,' she replied, and waited while he purchased a couple of ice-creams.

It took him much less time to demolish his ice-cream than it took Kendra to dispose of hers, and she still hadn't finished it when they reached his car. She was making a concentrated effort to down the rest of it, though, when she suddenly became aware of his eyes on her.

'What...?' she enquired, looking questioningly across at him, but thought she read the answer in the look which was all at once there in his eyes. 'No,' she said, but his head was already coming closer. Her only recourse was to move her head out of range. Costas's kiss landed on her cheek, but her clipped, 'Don't do that again,' left him in no doubt that his amorous advances were not being favourably received.

At once Costas was contrite. 'I've offended you?' he enquired, the amorous look at once gone from his eyes, to be replaced by a puppy-like plea for forgiveness.

Having formed the view that although Costas was about her own age he had a lot of growing up to do, Kendra was loath to tell him that she was not offended for fear he might aim another kiss at her.

'Let's get back to Athens, shall we?' she suggested, hoping that her light tone would convey that she wanted to forget the incident.

'You *are* offended!' Costas cried, as if he could not bear to live with himself. 'I've spoiled this day for you,' he went on, and sounded so dramatic to Kendra's ears that she was suddenly more amused than anything.

'Oh, Costas,' she said helplessly, and, having to play his game when he still looked tragic, 'I promise you I've loved every minute of this day—especially Delphi,' she tacked on. 'But now I think...'

'You will forgive me for trying to steal a kiss?'

What could she say? 'Of course,' she smiled, but only to discover that she was going to have to prove that she had forgiven him when he told her,

'I know a very pleasant place for dinner. Please allow me to prove I'm trustworthy by permitting me to take you there,' he pleaded.

'But—won't your father expect us back?' Kendra demured.

'No, no, I'm certain,' Costas told her urgently. 'Just as I'm sure that he understands we will dine outside of my home, I'm sure he would prefer that I drive slowly and show you some more of our Greek countryside.' Quickly he consulted his watch. 'It has gone five o'clock now,' he stated, 'which means that there is not much more than an hour of daylight left. Are you not going to let me make amends for my boorish behaviour?' he asked with dramatically sad eyes.

Again Kendra saw that there was only one course open to her. She took it. She laughed. 'You're the giddy limit,' she told him.

Instantly Costas was all smiles. 'I don't know what the giddy limit is, but it sounds as though it's something nice.'

This time when he had his car started he drove more slowly, and suddenly Kendra was starting to be a lot happier than she had been. She was on holiday and was beginning to enjoy it.

She was still much dazed that they could be so high up in what appeared to be range after range of mountains, and yet still see the sea below, when they started to drive through acres and acres of olive trees. Minutes later they had descended to the pretty little sea-port of Itea.

Where they were when Costas decided to stop for dinner, though, Kendra had no idea, but it was dark when he pulled his sports car up in front of a well-illuminated hotel.

Inside the hotel they were efficiently directed to the dining-room where they exchanged smiles when Costas ordered an English-type pork chop, potatoes and peas, whereas Kendra went Greek, and decided on *dolmades* for a starter, followed by *souvlakia*, which sounded very foreign, but which turned out to be charcoal-cooked lamb. Both she and Costas were served with a side salad.

Kendra did not know if it was general in Greece, but in this particular hotel they were given plenty of time in which to tackle each course, no one appearing in the smallest hurry for them to eat and leave.

The time was getting on, she realised, when the *baklava* which she had ordered for her dessert appeared. But, since Costas did not seem in any way anxious, she relaxed as she cut into her honey and nut pastry, and calculated that, driving at the speed which he would drive now that it was too dark for her to see anything of the scenery, they would still be home before midnight.

Though when their desserts were finished, and he seemed more inclined to linger over a second cup of coffee than to return to Athens, she began to feel a niggle of anxiety.

'More coffee for you too, Kendra?' he enquired, and when she shook her head, he seemed to suddenly sense some of her anxiety. 'You are not worried that I'll misbehave myself again?' he asked quickly. 'Have you not seen how ashamed I...?'

'I'm not worried on that score at all,' Kendra told him truthfully. 'It's just that I'm—a little concerned that everyone will be in bed when we get back, and that we might risk waking up the whole household...' She did not have to go further. As if to give her more evidence that he was the most trustworthy of beings, Costas straight away called for their bill.

They were in the hotel car park when he told her confidently, 'We'll be back in Athens in no time—I know a short cut!'

Oh, lord, Kendra muttered under her breath, her thoughts given over to the family joke about her father and the way, whenever he took a short cut, it always took him twice as long. Indeed, many were the times, when he went out on his own, that her mother would laugh, 'Take the long way home, dear!'

In the event, Costas's short cut was dogged by a double calamity. Not only did his short cut include a couple of wrong turns which took them miles out of their way, but, during the endeavour to find the right road, his car just guzzled up fuel. They were well off a main road, with not so much as a house in sight, let alone a garage, when the car ran out of petrol.

'I swear I'm out of petrol, I honestly am!' Costas beseeched her to believe him when he realised why his car had stopped and was refusing to be coaxed another inch.

'I believe you,' Kendra told him calmly, feeling inwardly a little worried at the lateness of the hour, but not seeing that she was going to do a scrap of good by throwing a panic.

'I wouldn't have had this happen for anything,' he told her sincerely. 'I promise you, you've nothing to be frightened of.'

'I'm not frightened,' Kendra told him, and spent the next couple of minutes convincing him that that was so, and another couple of minutes calming him down.

Only then was Costas able to think constructively. His thinking yielded little, though, except that he could not remember passing a petrol filling station recently, and that, in any case, he certainly would not leave her alone while he went looking for one.

'I'll come with you,' she volunteered, but Costas didn't care for that idea either.

'We'll wait,' he said. 'Another car is bound to come along shortly.'

Another car did come along. It fact, in due time, several cars came along, but none that paid any heed to Costas's attempts to flag them down. Grateful that she had thought to bring a lightweight jacket with her, even then Kendra felt chilled to her marrow when, what seemed like hours later, the driver of an approaching car did stop.

Hoping that the driver would be kind enough to allow Costas to syphon off sufficient petrol to enable them to get to a petrol pump, she was greatly relieved when after a brief conversation the man went to the boot of his car and, in exchange for some notes, handed Costas his spare can of petrol. More, it seemed the man was able to direct them on to the road which they should have been on.

From then, and as soon as Costas had found the right road, he wasted no time in getting them back to Athens. Even so, though, the time was going on for two in the morning when they finally pulled up at the villa.

Costas renewed his apologies that his car had run out of petrol as they walked up the garden path, and Kendra tried to make him see that anyone could have run out of petrol in the circumstances. But when he seemed determined to continue to wear sackcloth and ashes, all she could do was to refer to how well the rest of their outing had gone.

They were just entering the house, when, as she was telling him, 'I thought Delphi was absolutely out of this world,' Kendra suddenly stopped dead. One thing she had not anticipated was that they should arrive home to a reception committee. But, as her startled glance went from a furious-looking Eugene to the taller and equally furious-looking man standing near him, she realised that a reception committee was what they had come home to—a hostile reception committee, at that!

'Costas!' Eugene called his name angrily, and in fact seemed so angry with his son that he forgot to speak in English in Kendra's company, and let go at him with a stream of Greek. Only when Costas tried to answer him in English did he seem to recollect that she could not understand. And then it was when, looking very much as though he would like to box his ears, Eugene issued a short command, which seemed to Kendra to be an order that Costas should follow him, and both father and son headed off in the direction of Eugene's study.

Sensing that Costas was in for a short, sharp wigging from his father, it was in Kendra's mind to put in a good word for Costas, and she made an instinctive move to go after them. Suddenly, though, she was prevented from doing anything of the kind. Suddenly her way was blocked when, hostile, dark and forbidding, Damon Niarkos stepped in front of her.

'Leave him alone!' he grated harshly, as she looked up at him in some surprise.

'Don't be...' she started to retort shortly, but she was cut off as she went to step smartly round him when Damon caught hold of her arm and swung her round, his expression murderous.

'I said leave him alone!' he snarled. 'You've caused enough upset tonight without...'

'*I've* caused enough upset!' Kendra exclaimed, angry herself by that time—just who did this woman-handling Damon Niarkos think he was? 'How?' she charged. 'What have *I* done?'

'Eugene has enough to worry over without you leading his son astray!' Damon gritted, his jaw jutting at a furious angle.

'Leading him astray!' Kendra choked. 'My g-giddy aunt!' she spluttered, her anger spiralling. 'He's twenty-two!' she exclaimed, and grew more and more enraged as Damon's accusation sank in. She had never led anyone astray in her life!

Her growing rage didn't stop at mere fury, though, but was to go into overdrive when, taking another angry step closer, Damon Niarkos hurled at her, 'He might be the same age as you in years, Miss Jephcott, but from what I've seen of you I'd say that when it comes to "adult relationships" you're years ahead in experience!'

For a split second, Kendra did not believe her hearing. No one had *ever* spoken to her like that before! In the next split of a second, though, she was so wildly angry that Damon Niarkos could speak to her thus, that she was in no mood to ask him to repeat it to see if she *had* heard him correctly. In the next split of that same second, all hell had broken loose within her.

'Why, you...!' she hissed, and as her hand began to sting, she saw the mark her hand had made on the side of his face. Only then did she appreciate that she had lost control completely and—that she had hit him!

But, if *she* had lost control, as the one word, *'Theos!'* escaped in an angry sound from between his teeth and his hands snaked out for her Kendra realised that Damon himself was also a hair's breadth from losing his self-control.

For a numbed moment or two as with a demoniacal look on his face he began to draw her inexorably closer, Kendra had no idea what he intended to do. But suddenly, as his head began to come nearer, so she sensed more than anything that her punishment was not to be a slap of retaliation.

His well-shaped mouth was over hers before full comprehension of what he was about had dawned on her.

And then it was too late. For by then the hands that had been on her arms and which had been drawing her closer were suddenly all the way round her slender form, and all at once she was being hauled up close against him.

'No!' she protested, when she managed to free her mouth, his kiss, after what he had said, adding insult to injury. But with lightning speed he had found her mouth and had again taken possession.

Struggling to break his hold, Kendra ignored the warmth that suddenly began to surge in her body. She had been frozen in Costas's car. She had... But this wasn't Costas! Costas had tried to kiss her, but she hadn't wanted Costas to kiss her.

Suddenly, though, Damon's anger seemed to start to leave him. Suddenly, his hands at her back began to make gentle soothing patterns. Suddenly Kendra was losing the will to fight. Damon's lips were still over hers when, without her known volition, she began to cease struggling. This wasn't Costas, she repeated to herself—it was Damon. She hadn't wanted Costas to kiss her—but... Damon's mouth over her own became more gentle, and all at once Kendra knew that she wanted Damon to kiss her.

Clinging to him, her body moulded against his, she lifted her arms up and around his shoulders, and as Damon kissed her, so she returned his kiss.

The sound of the study door opening followed by muted Greek voices was to bring her suddenly to her senses. Stunned, as much by her behaviour as by anything, she pulled her head back and thought she read in Damon's expression that he was pretty shaken too.

'I...!' she gasped, and heard footsteps. Hurriedly, she pulled out of Damon's arms. 'G-goodnight,' she choked, and, too confused to see anybody else that night—she fled.

CHAPTER FIVE

MORNING arrived before Kendra was ready for it. She had been extremely late in going to bed, but it had still taken her an age to get off to sleep. As a consequence, she had overslept.

Pattering to the bathroom to get showered and dressed, Kendra could not get out of her mind the heated way in which she had responded to Damon.

She was glad she had missed going down to breakfast, and she owned that she needed more time before she saw Costas, or indeed his father, again.

Keeping to her bedroom, she set about making her bed and tidying round, finding that she needed to keep her mind as occupied as she could. But these small tasks, she discovered, were no help whatsoever in stemming memory after memory which just insisted on returning.

Determinedly she shook all recall of Damon's kisses from her and chose instead to remember how it had come about that, his insults more than she could take, she had lashed out at him. He had earned that slap, though, she thought, and started to get angry again. It was enough that he should take it upon himself to order her to leave Costas alone, let alone accuse her of leading him astray! From what she had seen of Costas's flirtatiousness, it would have been the other way around had she, instead of nipping his advances in the bud, given him the smallest encouragement.

Kendra's fury against Damon went up another notch when she dwelt on how Costas had never appeared to be some naïve boy to her, but seemed a young man who was not lacking in experience with the opposite sex. Which, since Damon had accused her of being *years ahead* of him in experience, made her sound worse than some—tart!

Kendra was doubly glad she had hit him then. In her view he'd more than had it coming. He had been disagreeable from the *very first*. Even his best friend, if he had one, she considered, could not have accused him of brimming over with charm at Faye and Eugene's wedding. Kendra realised then that the slap she had served him had most likely been on its way to him since then.

When, shortly afterwards, though, she started to dwell again on how Damon had reacted to that first ever slap she had delivered to any man, she decided that she needed to go and see her cousin.

She went hurriedly into Faye's suite of rooms and tried to eject thoughts of Damon Niarkos from her head by wondering if Faye knew anything of Eugene's anger last night.

She did not have to wait long to find out, for Faye was sitting up in bed and, dispensing with even a 'Good morning', 'Well, you've certainly livened up the old homestead,' she said as soon as she saw her.

'You've—heard?' Kendra enquired.

'I've had a blow by blow account,' Faye replied, inadvertently causing her to flinch yet again, even though Kendra was sure that no one but herself and Damon knew about the blow she had struck him.

'By the sound of it,' Kendra remarked, feeling a shade disgruntled, 'I'm the cause of all the upset!'

'Not at all!' Faye laughed, and, when she could see that Kendra could find nothing to laugh at, 'Oh, don't throw a moody, love,' she said, causing Kendra's eyes to widen at the cheek, the unfairness of it—when she had done nothing but cope with Faye's moods since she had got there! 'Part of the reason for Eugene being so rattled last night was you and your reputation, I'll agree that far...'

'Eugene was concerned about my reputation?'

'Of course!' exclaimed Faye. 'The other part was that, because Costas is such a mad-head when he's behind the wheel of that sports car of his, he was worried on that score too.'

'Is Costas prone to car accidents, then?' Kendra asked what seemed to her a perfectly natural question in the circumstances.

'He leads a charmed life in that direction,' Faye told her. 'Though Eugene is such a worrier when it comes to the people he cares for that I'm sure he's convinced that Costas's luck will run out any day now. Anyhow, when you weren't home by midnight he was certain that Costas must have been showing off at the wheel simply because he had you with him.'

'We took a wrong turn or two, and then ran out of petrol,' Kendra explained.

'I know. Costas told Eugene all about it,' Faye responded. 'Anyhow, when I tried to tell Eugene that I was sure that you were both all right, though not convinced, he then started to be furious that by keeping you out so late—for the whole of the night, so far as we knew then—it was tantamount to dishonouring you while you were a guest in his home.'

'Good lord!' Kendra exclaimed.

'That's more or less what I said,' laughed Faye. 'Anyway, Eugene went on hot and strong about how we should be guarding your reputation, and what he was going to do to Costas, his own son, who was showing all signs of being careless of it.'

'Poor Costas,' Kendra sighed, and the two of them fell silent for some moments, until Kendra just had to murmur an idle-sounding, 'I was surprised to see Damon here. Had he been dining with you and Eugene?'

Faye shook her head. 'When Eugene began to get really worried about the two of you, he rang Damon on the off-chance that you and Costas might have gone there for some reason.'

That did not explain to Kendra what Damon was doing at Eugene's villa, but she lost any chance to find out more—not that it was in any way important in any case—when Faye went on to tell her that Eugene had insisted she go to bed and get her rest and that he would wait up to have a 'quiet' word with Costas when he did eventually arrive home.

'I'm so sorry there's been all this upset,' Kendra apologised.

'Don't worry about it,' her cousin replied. 'I'll admit I didn't get a wink of sleep until I heard that you were both home safe—but do you know what?'

'What?' Kendra obliged.

'I think that disturbed nights agree with me. I think I'll get up and take a look at the garden.'

At first Kendra was stunned. She had spent ages coaxing and cajoling Faye to leave her rooms before her usual evening time, all without result. And now... Kendra's next reaction was to send her a beaming smile.

'Allow me to run your bath for you, Kyria Themelis,' she said formally.

'*Efharisto*, Thespinis Jephcott,' Faye laughed.

'*Parakalo,*' Kendra grinned.

An hour later, the two of them were sitting in the garden taking advantage of the warm October morning. A smiling Sybil had been out to check if they wanted for anything, and a smiling Medea had brought them tea and pastries and, with only one fly in her ointment, namely Damon Niarkos, Kendra felt near enough happy.

She was feeling most definitely in a holiday mood, at any rate, as she sunned herself and talked over all manner of things with her cousin. 'I need, fairly desperately, to get to a bank as soon as I can,' she mentioned to her at one point.

'You're short of cash?' Faye had queried, and not waiting for her reply, 'I've plenty of money. I can . . .'

'I want my own,' Kendra cut her off.

'You would!' Faye exclaimed, and they both burst out laughing.

They were both in the middle of a giggle over something quite inconsequential when, for once, father and son arrived home together.

'My dear!' Eugene exclaimed, sounding amazed to see the wife whom he had expected to be up in their private apartments actually up and dressed, and down in the garden.

Kendra had had it in mind to make some sort of apology to Eugene for any anxiety he had suffered on her behalf the previous evening. But the expression on his face as he beheld his wife was such a delight that every thought of apologising went out of her head.

Then it was too late to apologise, for, pausing only to courteously wish Kendra the most cheerful of greetings, Eugene, after questioning his wife on how long she had been sitting in the garden, was telling her that she must now rest, and was escorting her indoors.

'*You* still like me, don't you?' Costas asked Kendra as soon as they were alone.

'Who could help it?' she smiled, as he slipped into the lounger which Faye had just vacated.

'My father is one such,' Costas complained.

'He loves you very much, and you know it,' Kendra told him severely.

At once Costas shed his dramatics and brightened visibly. 'I know it,' he agreed. 'But it's going to be a tiring time for me, being what—I think you call—on my best behaviour. Do you know,' he shed his bright look to complain, 'that although my car just adores to fly, when I spotted my father driving a few cars in front of me just now I dared not overtake him as I would have done yesterday.'

'Shame,' Kendra laughed, and was in no doubt at all that this time next week Costas would have forgotten whatever sort of lecture his father had given him, which must have included words on speeding, and that it just wouldn't occur to him to tuck in behind his father's car and stay there.

Costas grinned, and chatted with her for ten minutes or so, then he went to freshen up for lunch.

It was over their meal, with Faye and Eugene keeping to their habit of dining in their private suite, that Costas referred to the telling off which his father had given him last night.

Having told her more or less what Faye had told her, including Eugene's anger that a son of his should risk compromising a guest under his roof by keeping her out so late and, for all he knew, not intending to bring her back at all, Costas ended, 'Mercifully, my father kept it fairly short and sharp.'

'You explained to him, though, how we ran out of petrol.'

'My father has no understanding of such a situation,' Costas replied. 'According to him, the least I could have done was to have telephoned.' He grinned again, as he added, 'Even when I told him that we were stranded miles away from a telephone, he was still of the opinion that I should have telephoned him!'

Kendra returned to the garden with Costas after her meal. She spent most of the afternoon out of doors with him, and returned to her room only once when she donned her swimsuit and went back to take advantage of the pool. She had enjoyed her day when eventually she went up to her room to bathe and wash her hair, and get ready for dinner.

They normally dined about nine, and it was going on for half past eight when Kendra stepped into a full-skirted dress of coffee and red splodgy-patterned cotton. When she went downstairs, however, she found that her host was the sole occupant of the sitting-room.

'Hello, Eugene,' she smiled, and, encouraged when he greeted her warmly and returned her smile, she ventured, 'I wanted to have a private word with you to tell you how sorry I am about last night, and that—that there was really nothing Costas could...'

'You don't have to apologise,' Eugene interrupted her, and with some charm, he told her, 'Costas has explained everything to me, and I, perhaps, have acquainted him with certain courtesies in such matters. But,' he went on, 'more important than my son's thoughtless behaviour is the wonder that you have performed in getting my wife out into the garden this morning.'

'Oh, it was Faye's idea,' Kendra quickly told him. 'I didn't do anyth...'

'You have been working away ever since you arrived,' he insisted. 'I know that.' He paused, then, smiling again, he went on, 'Just as I know that you have a small problem.'

The only problem which Kendra would have said she had on her horizon just then was the thorn in her side,

Damon Niarkos. But, since she did not think that Eugene could be meaning him, she queried, 'I have?'

'Faye tells me that you're short of money, but will not allow her to lend you any,' Eugene answered. 'And I can see from your solemn expression that I shall risk offending you if I make the same offer. So,' he announced, a teasing look coming to his eyes, 'I think the next best thing will be for me to take you to my bank in the morning.'

'Would you?' Kendra asked, her smile soon coming out of hiding at the thought of being solvent once more, and with her own funds.

'It will be my pleasure,' he said formally. 'I will wait for you and bring you back h...'

'Oh, there's no need for that!' Kendra exclaimed, not wanting to keep him from his office. 'I can get a taxi back, I'm sure. Besides,' she said when he looked doubtful, 'I'd like to buy some postcards to send home, and,' she grinned, 'I wouldn't at all mind taking a look at the shops.'

'Ah, the eternal woman,' he said, and suddenly, he hesitated just as though a thought had at that moment struck him. 'Would you mind... Could I ask...' He broke off, and then brought out, 'Would you find time to perhaps purchase some little gift for Faye? Something which maybe you, as another woman, would know that she would appreciate?'

'Of course,' Kendra told him, even though she was aware that Faye lacked for nothing. 'I'd be delighted,' she had just added, when she thought of something which Faye did need, but which Eugene had clearly not noticed. 'In fact,' she said, 'I think I've a very good idea of something which might be the very thing.'

In next to no time, while being as loyal to her cousin as she could, Kendra was outlining to a startled Eugene that Faye had the tiniest hang-up about maternity clothes. Briefly she told him that Faye could not go on wearing the same few dresses until the baby was born, because before too long even those few would be bursting at the seams.

'But you must buy for her whatever she needs!' he exclaimed, and, looking devastated to think that he had neglected his wife, 'Why did I not see for myself that she needs new clothes?' he asked, his voice full of contrition.

'Probably because it's only recently that she's had to give up wearing her more fitted outfits,' Kendra told him, certain that Eugene loved Faye so much that he was content just to see her and to be with her, that he had no mind to notice that she had only three dresses which she could get into.

They talked for a few minutes more on the subject. But while Eugene seemed all in favour of Kendra's purchasing a whole new wardrobe for his wife, Kendra thought it would be a better idea to introduce only one garment initially and to see how that was received. By then Eugene was agreeable to anything she said, and he was in the middle of talking charge accounts when suddenly he halted, and started to question her lack of any Greek.

'Perhaps it would be easier if I came with you?' he suggested.

'I'm sure I can manage on my own,' Kendra told him stoutly, and realised that she must have sounded totally confident about that, for in the next minute Eugene was extracting his wallet from his lightweight suit, and was telling her,

'I think it will be less complicated for you if you settle your transaction with cash.' So saying, he handed her a whole fistful of money. Kendra was standing holding what seemed to be thousands and thousands of drachmas when he said, 'You must let me know if that is not enough, and I'll . . .' when something over her shoulder attracted his attention, and he smiled and broke off.

The money was still in her hands when she turned to see what he was smiling at, and at the sight of the tall man who had come silently into the room in time to see Eugene give her the contents of his wallet Kendra went a sudden and abrupt scarlet.

Shaken to see Damon there, all she could think of in those initial moments of seeing him again was the passionate kiss they had exchanged. Her heart was racing wildly when she saw his glance go from her eyes to her mouth, and leave the embarrassed colour of her face to go down to her hands.

The colour was still high in her face from the memory of his kisses when her eyes followed his, and on a gasp of breath she realised how it must look to him. Realising that she must look as guilty as hell and every bit as though she had asked Eugene to give her some money, Kendra proved her guilt by quickly following through with what just had to look like a guilty reaction, by rapidly stuffing the money deep down into the pocket in the skirt of her dress and out of sight.

Abruptly, though not before she had seen the crystals of ice forming in his eyes, Damon switched his gaze and, as if nothing untoward had happened, she heard him greet Eugene and, as courteously as ever speaking in English, he added, 'Rhodeia and I were passing when I remembered a message I have for Costas.' And, turning smoothly to her, 'Good evening,' he murmured politely.

'Good evening,' Kendra murmured in return, but she did not have to wait long to find out who Rhodeia was, because just then Faye, Costas and a most stunning-looking dark-haired woman of about thirty all came into the sitting-room together.

Greek mingled with English for a minute or two, as Kendra gained an impression that Damon had left the Greek beauty in the hall while he went looking for Costas and that Faye had come down the stairs, with Costas joining them pretty much at the same time. Then Damon was in front of her and was formally performing the introductions. He had got as far as introducing the woman as Thespinis Rhodeia Stassinopoulos when suddenly Kendra was coping with shock.

She was aware that her colour was high again, and hoped with all she had that everyone would conclude that it was from consternation of having made a complete mess-up of the woman's surname when, shaking hands with her, she endeavoured to tack on 'Miss Stassinopoulos' to the end of her formal 'How do you do.'

As jealousy swamped Kendra she wanted to hate the handsome woman, but she found that she could not hate her when the woman smiled and invited, 'Perhaps you had better call me Rhodeia. I may call you Kendra?' she enquired.

'Of course,' Kendra smiled back, and fought with all she had to hide the fact that she had just discovered why Damon Niarkos had had such a peculiar effect on her from the beginning.

Jealousy bit again when, his message having been passed on to Costas apparently, Damon refused the offer of refreshment, saying that he had a table booked for dinner.

To her relief, they did not stay above another minute longer. Kendra was trying to look as if she was hardly aware that he was there anyway, and had moved to stand next to Costas, when, his glance taking in everyone in the room, Damon made his farewells and escorted his woman-friend from the room.

Kendra had no idea what she ate at dinner that night. Nor could she wait for dinner to be done with. She wanted, needed, to be alone. She had just realised that she was in love with Damon Niarkos and she badly needed to be by herself so that she could try and think how best to cope with that fact. Because, leaving aside his belief that she was some money-grubbing female—and what had it looked like when he had come in, but that Eugene was giving her a hand-out?—one look at the elegant, soignée type of woman whom he chose to date was enough to show that she hadn't got a chance.

Kendra eventually went up to her room, to grow more and more unhappy with her thoughts. For, as minute followed minute, she was recalling that she was the only one to whom Damon had introduced Rhodeia Stassinopoulos. From that, she could only conclude that the others already knew her. Which had to mean that this was not Damon's first date with her. Which, in turn, could quite well mean that Rhodeia Stassinopoulos was Damon's steady woman-friend.

Her love for Damon too newly realised, her feelings too tender, Kendra knew that if Damon was seriously involved, she did not want to know. She had felt jealousy like a physical pain, and she did not want any more of it. She was aware that she would not be asking Faye any questions about either of them and, more than anything just then, Kendra wanted to go home to England.

She was glad to see Friday morning arrive, and she was out of bed and was bathed and dressed early. She was prompt down to breakfast too, but she discovered that she was not the only one who had had a bad night when Eugene came and shared a cup of coffee with her and Costas and told her, 'I'm afraid I cannot take you to my bank this morning as I promised. Faye was sick during the night and I will stay with her until the doctor comes.'

'She's ill!' Kendra exclaimed in alarm.

'She says not. She says that she is feeling well again this morning, but I would still like her physician to see her,' Eugene said, and went on to ask Costas if he would take Kendra into town for him.

'With enormous pleasure, of course,' Costas immediately agreed.

'Kendra will not want you to stay with her—just to take her to the bank,' Eugene told him.

'But how will she get back?'

'By taxi,' Eugene replied, and turning to her he handed her what she assumed must be his personal card, for she could make nothing of the Greek characters. 'If you show this to the taxi driver, he will bring you straight here,' he told her, and stayed only to wish her to have an enjoyable time, leaving her and Costas to finish breakfast while he returned to sit with his wife.

'Great!' Costas exclaimed.

'What's great?' asked Kendra.

'I've a perfect excuse for not rushing into the office this morning,' he replied.

'You're incorrigible!'

'If I knew what that meant, I'd probably agree with you,' Costas grinned.

When later he drove her into the centre of Athens, Kendra saw for herself what a nightmare the traffic was. 'You're never going to be able to park,' she told him. 'Just drop me off where you can, and I'll find my own way to a bank.'

'Are you sure?' Costas asked.

'Positive,' Kendra told him, and quickly got out of his car when, chancing his luck, he pulled up in Omonia

Square. Making it safely to the pavement, she turned to wave to him, then set about finding a bank.

After some minutes she found a bank and went in, to discover that she could get some currency by using a credit card. She had to wait, however, while her credit card was checked out, and soon her interest in all that was going on had evaporated and thoughts of Damon had entered her head.

It was no longer a mystery to her why she had felt at Delphi as though something was missing—Damon had not been there. She had no need to question it; she now knew that Delphi would have been every bit as magical as she had found the Acropolis—had Damon been by her side.

'Efharisto!' she thanked the bank clerk when he eventually handed her back her credit card, plus the drachmas she had purchased.

'Parakalo!' he smiled, his eyes lingering on her long blonde hair.

Kendra stayed inside the bank while she put her money away, then she walked outside—and got the shock of her life. For she bumped straight into none other than Damon Niarkos!

Shaken speechless, her heart pounding furiously, all she could hope was that Damon would read her shock as only normal surprise at bumping into him so unexpectedly.

'H-hello,' she managed to stammer a greeting, and, suspecting that he had some business inside the bank, she moved away from the doorway.

When Damon too moved to one side too, though—the same side—she looked up. She saw that there was not a glimmer of a smile on his face as he stared down at her.

'May I take you for some refreshment—some coffee?' he enquired evenly, however.

Had he smiled, Kendra thought, even while knowing that he had a low opinion of her, she might have accepted his offer. But he did not smile, and suddenly she was fed up to her back teeth with his Greek good manners which decreed that, even if he had no liking for her, since he had accidentally bumped into her in the street he could nevertheless do none other in public than show her the common courtesy which a guest of his distant relative required of him.

'Thank you, but no,' she replied primly, a dent appearing in her English good manners as her English pride made her voice a degree on the cool side.

She saw Damon's chin jut an arrogant fraction, but she remained that shade haughty herself when, his good manners staying with him, he said, 'You have obviously finished your business in the bank. If you will not permit me to give you coffee, then you must allow me to give you a lift back to Eugene's villa.'

Realising that, since she had been coming out of the bank when they had met, it was fairly clear that her business inside was done, Kendra was still intent on, figuratively speaking, cutting off her nose in a big way.

'It's very kind of you to offer, Damon,' she said pleasantly, wanting to bite off her tongue at the slip which had let her add his name, 'but I've some shopping I want to do.' He had never looked particularly pleased to see her anyway, she thought, but as his expression went icy, Kendra's pride made her even more haughty. 'I'll take a taxi when my shopping's done,' she told him aloofly, and saw that Damon thought he had done all that good manners required of him.

'Then I'll wish you good day,' he said curtly, and Kendra started walking.

Wretched man, she fumed angrily, and, her equilibrium well and truly upset by the encounter, she gave not a thought to where she was going.

Pride helped her over the next five minutes when, already starting to regret that she had turned down both his offers, she realised that he had not been a bit put out to have either offer refused anyway. What had made him go icy on her, she suddenly realised, was that he must have recalled seeing Eugene giving her all that money last night and, with her talking of shopping, had thought that she could not wait to get to the shops to spend it.

Wanting to hate Damon because, despite seeing her coming out of a bank, he would more readily believe she would prefer to spend someone else's money than her own, Kendra paused to take in her surroundings. She discovered that her feet had instinctively brought her to a very smart shopping area. To shop for a maternity outfit, and in a foreign language, was just what she needed to take Damon Niarkos out of her head, she decided.

Walking along until she spied one likely-looking shop in particular, Kendra went in and to her pleased surprise discovered that the assistant spoke English.

Three quarters of an hour later Kendra left the store with the most exquisite suit which was just the exact blue colour of Faye's eyes. Thrilled with her purchase, she had realised that, even if she had winced at the price, Eugene would not wish her to select anything but the best for Faye.

During the next hour Kendra found her way back to Omonia Square. She had wandered around and noted the trolley-buses and the hot-chestnut man in Stadiou Street, and, in the same street, she had stood and admired a dress in the window of a store called Matzoris, but all the time Damon was in her head. She was in the act of buying some postcards from a kiosk when she thought she saw Damon again. But it was not him. In fact, as her heartbeats steadied again as the man came nearer, she could see that he was nothing at all like Damon. But it was then that Kendra realised that she must leave Greece.

Espying a taxi pulled up in the choked traffic, she dashed over and showed the driver the card which Eugene had given her. What the driver said, she had no idea, but the nodding of his head told her more than words, and with a hasty *'Efharisto,'* as the traffic began to move again, she quickly got in.

She did not want to leave Greece, she knew that. Since it was Damon's home, she felt that she never wanted to leave. But leave she must, it was the only way. Her thoughts were on her decision and how it would be much better if she went at once and forgot all about her second week's holiday, when suddenly, as the taxi halted at some traffic lights, a man appeared out of nowhere, exchanged a few words with the driver, and came and got into the front passenger seat. Damon went temporarily out of her head at this procedure, but he was soon back again, only to depart briefly when, money exchanging hands, the taxi driver stopped to let his extra fare out.

Damon left her mind again when at the villa she paid and tipped the driver, and went in to find Eugene having a word with the man who did the garden.

'Ah, Kendra!' Eugene smiled as he saw her, and he went with her into the hall of the villa where he enquired after her morning and she handed him her purchase for Faye and what little change there was from the money he had given her.

'I think she'll like it,' Kendra told him, bearing in mind that Faye had stated an aversion to maternity clothes. 'How is she?' she asked. 'Has the doctor been?'

Eugene nodded, and told her contentedly, 'Faye has recovered from her indisposition of the night, and is much more comfortable. In fact, Dr Kostikos tells me that she is much improved from the last time he saw her.'

'Oh, that's good!' Kendra replied in pleased exclamation.

'It is, is it not?' Eugene said, but went on to stagger her when he added, 'Which has made me think, after he went, that since Faye has been much more cheerful since the time you came to us, perhaps you will do me the big favour of staying with us until after our baby is born.'

'I...w...' Dumbfounded, Kendra looked into Eugene's earnest soft brown puppy-dog eyes. Oh, lord, she thought, and just knew that it just was not the time to tell him that she had been thinking in terms of shortening her holiday, not extending it. 'But what about my job?' she asked, pulling the delaying tactic question out of the hat.

'You need not worry about that,' Eugene was quick to tell her. 'Naturally, I shall not condone you being—er—out of pocket, for doing this favour for m...'

'I couldn't take money from you!' Kendra quickly cut him off. But she was even more staggered when she realised from Eugene's sudden beaming smile that he had taken her exclamation to mean that she had agreed to stay.

'Thank you, Kendra,' he said sincerely, and as she stared at him in stunned silence, 'I shall be eternally grateful to you,' he added. 'And now,' he went on before she had found her voice, 'I must take this gift to my love and hope to see her sunny smile.'

Carrier bag in hand, he was half-way up the stairs when Kendra found her voice to protest, 'But...' But he did not hear her, and she watched him disappear round the bend of the staircase knowing that it had been cowardly of her not to tell him there and then that his idea was out of the question. She would definitely tell him the very next time that she saw him, though, she determined.

She returned to her room to freshen up, then went out into the garden to write her cards, realising as she did so that to write the cards was only a token gesture, because she would be home long before they were received.

She was still out in the garden, and there had not been another sign of Eugene, when Costas came home. 'I'll post your cards for you,' he volunteered when she told him that she had forgotten to buy stamps.

'I'll give you the money,' she said automatically and, she discovered, to Costas's amusement.

'I won't be bankrupt if I buy a few stamps,' he laughed, and was in a teasing if flirtatious humour then and throughout lunch.

Kendra did not see Eugene again until that evening. And then what was burning on her tongue to be said went temporarily from her mind. For Faye, wearing the suit she had selected for her, came into the sitting-room with him.

'You look fabulous!' Kendra could not refrain from saying as she refused a drink and Eugene went to pour himself one.

'Thanks to you,' Faye smiled, revealing that Eugene must have told her she had shopped for it. 'I look slimmer in this than I did in the dress I wore last night, don't you think?' Faye asked, as if she was still surprised by the fact.

'I think it was designed to help you feel good about yourself,' Kendra commented.

'It's certainly done that. I feel better than I did first thing, anyway,' said Faye, and went on to disclose that who had shopped for her suit was not the only thing Eugene had told her. 'Though it could be that your staying to keep me sane until this wretched business is over has a good deal to do with that,' she smiled. And while Kendra was bracing herself to tell her that Eugene had got it all wrong, she added, 'You will stay, won't you, love? You're not in any panic to rush back to England, are you?'

Kendra lay sleepless in her bed that night and wondered again at the mess she had got herself into. It should have been the simplest thing in the world to tell Faye that she could not stay—but she hadn't.

It was Faye's using the words, 'You're not in any panic to rush back to England, are you?' that had done it, of course. It hadn't been cowardice this time that had prevented her from saying what had to be said. It had been pride. Because she certainly was in a rush to get back to England, and whether that was panic or no, fear that Faye might question her on the subject had kept her quiet. Pride had decreed that no one should know any of why she wanted to make a bolt for it—not even her dear cousin.

CHAPTER SIX

THE weekend did not go well for Kendra. She had another week of her holiday to go and, after a great deal of thought, she had realised that if it would be beneficial to Faye she could do no other than remain in Greece for that second week.

It was one thing, though, to be certain that she was not going to give up her job to stay in Greece until after her cousin's baby was born, and quite another to acquaint either Faye or Eugene with that fact, she discovered.

She had got up on Saturday morning with what she must do fixed firmly in her mind. She had gone down the stairs and, with Costas nowhere to be seen, had breakfasted alone with her ears alert for the sound of Eugene's tread.

When she did hear his footsteps she went swiftly out into the hall, fearing that he might go out before she reached him. But Eugene had no intention of going anywhere that morning. One look at his worried face was enough to tell her that Faye was not well, and her rehearsed, 'I'm afraid I can't stay longer than Friday,' promptly evaporated unsaid.

'Is there anything I can do, Eugene?' she asked quickly instead.

'Dr Kostikos will be here shortly,' he replied, with a look of thanks that he had no need to explain anything. 'Would you go and stay with Faye while I try to find something to settle her?'

Kendra did not waste time on further words but went swiftly up the stairs and through the private sitting-room to the bedroom to where Faye, propped up on pillows, lay looking absolutely exhausted.

'Don't ever,' she gasped, as Kendra drew near to the bed, 'get pregnant.'

'I'll do my best,' Kendra promised, and, realising that there was nothing she could do and that Faye's morning sickness would have to take its course, she took her cousin's hand and looking down into her ashen face, saying as encouragingly as she could, 'You're more than half-way there; it won't be long now.'

'Thank God you'll be here to help it pass,' Faye sighed, and looked to be having such a battle against bursting into tears that Kendra just knew that right now was not the time to tell her what she had to be told.

Nor was the time right any other part of the weekend. Somehow, when it seemed to be taking Faye all her time not to give way to weak tears, Kendra just could not tell her. And, with Eugene looking so harassed, Kendra thought she had better leave it a day or two.

Going down to breakfast on Monday, Kendra was resolving that she was definitely going to break her news to them that day when Costas fell into step with her.

'Have you no smile for me?' he teased, peering into her solemn eyes.

'Who could be glum with you around?' she asked, and had to laugh when he took her remark as a compliment and preened himself.

There was no time for Costas to linger after breakfast, but when he had gone to his office Kendra wandered outside into the warm sun. She hoped that if Eugene was going to his office too that morning, she might get the chance to tell him that she could not extend her holiday by four months, and that she had never actually promised she would.

She had to wait some time to see him, though. But just when she had begun to think that he did not intend to go to work that day, she heard the sound of his footsteps. Fleet-footedly, she went to stand on the path he would use.

'Good morning, Kendra,' he smiled as soon as he spotted her.

'Good morning, Eugene,' she replied, and, making no move to step out of his way, she discovered that it was one thing to know what she was going to say before she saw him, but that now, seeing his kind but tired face, she was drenched in unwarranted guilt at what she had to tell him. 'I—wanted to see you,' she said, when it must have been obvious to him that she hadn't planted herself on the path in front of him just to wish him good morning. 'I—er—haven't had the chance before,' she forced herself on, 'but I wanted...'

'Ah!' he caught on. 'It has been a very distressing weekend, has it not?' And, making Kendra realise that he hadn't caught on at all to what she wanted to see him about, but that he had misunderstood her completely, 'You are, of course, most concerned about your cousin, so I must apologise that I have not informed you of what her doctor had to say.'

More guilt was heaped on Kendra as she considered how selfish she was in being more concerned about leaving Greece than about what the doctor had to say.

'It's nothing serious, is it?' she asked with a sudden appalled start. 'I thought it was just part of Faye's having a baby that...'

'It is, it is,' Eugene assured her quickly. 'But her doctor tells me that she does not help herself by staying inside the house all the time.'

'She came and sat in the garden on Thursday!' Kendra reminded him, a trifle stiffly.

'You don't have to defend Faye to me, loyal one,' he said gently, his kind smile breaking through. 'For me she can do no wrong. But when I had a few sharp words with her physician, he convinced me that Faye must get out more than just *into the garden*.'

'I—don't know how you're going to achieve that,' Kendra said slowly.

'Neither do I,' he replied, and, with a glance at his watch, 'I must try and think of something.'

Kendra stepped out of his way. 'We both will,' she told him, and he had gone down the path while she was still trying to think of a way of getting Faye out of doors.

Kendra was half-way up the stairs on her way to see her cousin when she stopped dead. She still hadn't told Eugene that she was leaving on Friday!

'How are you feeling?' she asked Faye as she went into her bedroom.

'Awful!' Faye grunted.

'What you need is to get out into the fresh air. How about a walk around the block?' Kendra suggested lightly.

'You're about as subtle as a sledge-hammer!' Faye told her sourly.

'You know, huh?'

'That that old fool Kostikos wants me to get away from the house for a few hours at least once a week? Yes, I know,' Faye said disagreeably, adding, 'And don't you tell me that you agree with him—I've had enough of that from Eugene.'

'Oh, dear,' Kendra sighed. 'You haven't quarrelled with Eugene?'

'Came close! He's been badgering at me all weekend to let him take me somewhere.' Faye sniffed and started to look weepy, though whether because she was feeling foul, or because she was upset at her near quarrel with her husband, Kendra did not know. What she did know was that, with Faye looking so unhappy, she just did not have the heart to tell her that she could not stay beyond Friday.

'So,' she said bracingly, 'suppose we get some wool and start to knit some little white things?'

As she had expected, Faye looked at her as though she had suddenly sprouted whiskers. 'Get lost, Kendra Jephcott,' she told her in no uncertain terms. But, as Kendra had hoped, the idea was so ludicrous to Faye that she just had to laugh, her unhappiness for the moment forgotten.

Faye got up for dinner that evening, but Kendra guessed that Eugene must have been badgering away at her again to let him take her out, because there was a decidedly strained air between the two of them. Kendra judged that this was definitely not the time to suddenly state that she was going to call the airport before all flights to England were booked up for Friday.

Neither Faye nor Eugene lingered downstairs after the meal. 'I think I'll go straight to bed, if no one minds,' Faye announced as soon as she had eaten sufficient from the dish of grapes in front of her.

'Will you excuse us?' Eugene asked Kendra and his son formally.

'Of course,' Kendra murmured and, like Costas, she remained at the table while Faye and Eugene left the room.

'A friend of mine took delivery of a new sports car today,' Costas told Kendra as soon as they had gone. 'Would you like to come with me to see it?'

With a fair idea that Costas and his friend would be standing for hours with their heads stuck under the bonnet of the new sports car, Kendra declined. 'It's kind of you to ask me, Costas,' she told him pleasantly, 'but I think I'll stay home.'

'You're sure?' he pressed.

'Positive,' she smiled.

'You'll have coffee with me in the *saloni* before I go?' he asked.

'Of course,' she said light-heartedly, and went with him to the sitting-room. Fifteen minutes afterwards, Costas went out. A few minutes later, though, she heard him come back. 'You forgot your car keys...?' Her voice tailed off, and her heart suddenly set up the most almighty clamouring. For, on looking up, she saw that it was not Costas! 'I thought you were...' Her voice tailed off again, and she hurriedly veiled her eyes so that Damon Niarkos should not read in them what it did to her to see him again.

'Since Costas was roaring off down the avenue as I pulled up,' Damon drawled, 'I rather think he has his car keys with him.'

Looking up at Damon, Kendra wished he would sit down—she was getting a crick in her neck. Alternatively, she wished that her legs felt strong enough so that she could stand—and maybe walk away from him. But even from the distance of several yards, even without touching her, Damon Niarkos had the effect of making her legs feel weak.

'Er—Faye and Eugene are upstairs,' she thought she had better tell him. 'I think they've retired for the night,' she added, and as her brain patterns started to sort themselves out she realised that since he had still come in when knowing that Costas was not there, he must have come to see Eugene.

'Your cousin is improved from her indisposition of the weekend?' he enquired politely.

'Yes, thank you,' Kendra replied, realising that he must have seen Eugene at some time during the day and that Eugene must have told him how poorly Faye had been.

Suddenly, though, Damon's politeness got through to her and, as alarm entered her being, she forgot all about Faye and Eugene. Trying not to panic she wondered instead, what with this family being so punctilious about manners and everything, in the absence of anyone else, was she expected to act as hostess to Damon? He was family, said one part of her brain—he's nevertheless waiting for you to invite him to sit down, said another.

'Would you care to take a seat, Damon?' she enquired, when she thought she had herself somewhere near collected.

'Thank you,' he murmured. Totally relaxed, he looked quite comfortable as he took his ease in the chair nearest to her.

Kendra hoped with all her heart that Damon could neither see nor guess at the mass of agitation she felt inside. But she was certain he would go in a minute and leave whatever business he had with Eugene until the morning, so, doing her best to appear as totally relaxed as Damon, Kendra smiled her best hostess smile, and offered, 'I'm afraid this coffee's cold, but it won't take a moment to get some fresh.'

She was still smiling while she waited for his polite refusal. How she managed to keep that smile in place as he accepted, when she had been sure that he would not, she could not have said.

Somehow, too, though unable to speak Greek and not having the first idea of how to go on when asking one of the maids for coffee, Kendra managed to retain a pleasant expression.

'If you'll excuse me,' she said gracefully, and caught hold of the coffee-pot with the intention of carrying it to the kitchen.

'Allow me,' Damon uttered smoothly, and before she could leave her chair, he had risen to move over to press the bell-push, which she had known all the time was set into the wall.

Blaming this love she had for him that she was suddenly turning into such a senseless person, Kendra was still striving to get herself more of one piece as Sybil came into the room. Kendra then felt that she hated him more than she loved him when as Sybil looked to him, the only other Greek speaker in the room, Damon directed the maid to her.

Ignoring him, Kendra smiled at the maid and, hoping that the word *'Kafé'* was pretty international, '*Kafé, parakalo*, Sybil,' she requested, and was relieved when without question or enquiry, Sybil smiled back at her and then left the room.

Praying that she would soon come back, that Damon would soon drink his coffee, and that he would soon go, Kendra realised that in the meantime she could not continue to ignore him. Fortunately though, Sybil must have had the coffee brewing, for in no time she was back with a tray and two cups and saucers, and it was only when she went out again that Kendra had to rack her brains for some innocuous topic of conversation.

'Costas has just gone to see a friend who's taken delivery of a new car today,' she said evenly as she passed Damon a cup of coffee and, to be polite, poured herself a cup.

'He didn't ask you to go with him?' Damon asked, a shade brusquely she thought, thinking so much for her idea that the subject of Costas was an innocuous one.

She was uncertain then whether to be annoyed that Damon still seemed to nurse the idea that she was setting her cap at Costas, or whether she should refute the idea that Costas might be ill-mannered to leave her to amuse herself at home.

'He did, actually,' she replied, and started to feel so mixed up that she didn't know what to think any more.

'But you refused?'

His tone was sharp still, and suddenly Kendra was starting to feel nettled. Suddenly she was certain that Damon Niarkos was more concerned that she did not go out with Costas than he was concerned that Costas might have been found wanting in manners.

'I've ample time before Friday in which to enjoy Costas's company, and to go out with him,' she replied, and could do nothing about the cool edge that had come to her voice.

'Something of a special nature happens on Friday?' Damon demanded to know.

'You'll be pleased to learn that I fly back to England on Friday,' she replied tartly.

'Does Eugene know of this?' was his next demand.

'Well, no,' she was forced to own, some of the heat leaving her. 'There hasn't been a convenient moment to...' Suddenly she halted. Just as suddenly, she was sure that there was a reason behind Damon's question. 'You know, don't you, that Eugene has asked me to stay on until after Faye's baby is born?'

Damon nodded, and set his empty coffee-cup down upon the table. 'He mentioned that he'd invited you to stay to cheer Faye in this troublesome time for her, and...' he broke off to give her a sharp look '...and,' he continued, 'that you had agreed.'

'I didn't ag... Well, I can't stay,' Kendra said bluntly. But panic suddenly hit her. Damon had the power to make her more cross than anyone she knew, but fear that he might somehow glean that her main reason for wanting so desperately to leave was because of her love for him made her add smartly, 'By Friday I'll have used up all my holiday allowance from my job, so I really have no alternative but to return so as to be back at my desk for nine on Monday morning...' Her voice faded when she saw Damon start to shake his head. 'What...?' she began.

'You might have a bit of a problem there,' he drawled casually.

'How do you mean?' she enquired, wondering if there was some sort of air-crew strike or something which would prevent her from flying home on Friday.

She was still not taking it in when Damon told her, 'You'd have a problem being at your desk next Monday, or any other Monday—for the simple reason that you no longer have a job at Sollis Refrigeration.'

'I no longer... Sollis Refriger....' Dumbly, Kendra stared at him. How did he know where she worked? What the dickens was he talking about! Hardly crediting her hearing, she soon found out.

'I had a list of calls to make to London this afternoon,' Damon informed her. 'It took little effort to add Sollis Refrigeration to my list.'

'Y-you rang—my firm!'

'Your ex-firm,' he smiled, his scowls, it seemed for the moment, a thing of the past.

'W-what d-do you...?' she spluttered.

'Mr Anderson was most understanding when I explained how, in the circumstances of your family needing you, you would not be returning to work for him.'

'You—he—Mr Anderson...' she gasped, knowing that as she had not told him where she worked, she had not told him her boss's name either. Though, of a certainty, he could not have so accurately chanced on both names. 'You've given in my notice!' she exclaimed, and as the import of that suddenly struck home, she was on her feet staring at him incredulously, her disbelief there in her rising voice as she charged, 'You actually had the *nerve*, the...the *utter gall*, to take it upon yourself to give in my notice!'

'I thought it would be easier if I did it for you,' Damon said pleasantly, getting to his feet too and revealing that when he cared to use it he also had charm—by the bootful.

'You thought!' Never had she so much as dreamed that anyone could, or would, do such a thing.

'Anderson spoke very highly of you, and seemed sorry to lose you,' he commented, looking every bit as though he was not aware that she was angry enough to go into orbit. 'Naturally, though, when he spoke of how busy the company was, I fully appreciated that he just couldn't afford to keep your job open for the six months you'll be away.' Six months! Kendra was still reeling, when Damon ended pleasantly, 'Anderson said he would advertise your job straight away.'

'How—*dare* you?' Kendra choked, only the memory of the retaliatory way he had kissed her the last time she had hit him preventing her from physically setting about him.

'I thought I was helping,' he smiled.

'You thought nothing of the kind!' she erupted furiously. 'I don't know why you did it, but it sure as hell wasn't with any idea of helping me! My godfathers!' she went storming on, taking no heed of the fact that his gaze was never wavering from the sparks flying in her angry green eyes. 'Have you any idea of what you've done?' And, not giving him chance to tell her if he had, 'You've taken away my right to do what *I* think best!

You've taken away from me a job I liked, a job I did well, a job that paid better than most. You've...'

'If it's the money that bothers you,' Damon cut in, his charm and seemingly good humour soon departing as that subject came up, 'then I'm certain Eugene will not see you short of...'

'It is *not* what I'm afraid of!' Kendra cut him off. 'And for your information, although I don't expect you to believe it,' she raged, 'I wouldn't take a penny from Eugene—or from any man!'

'*Theos!* You've changed!' Damon snarled, and suddenly, almost toe to toe as they stood, his chin jutted at an angry angle.

But Kendra was too furious to care how he looked. 'If you're referring to last Thursday, then had you arrived five minutes earlier you'd have heard Eugene and me discussing Faye's need for maternity clothes. Had you been there then,' she hurried on after taking an angry breath, 'you'd have known that the money he gave me was in order that I could purchase something for her when I went shopping the next day!' Kendra waited until she saw it register with Damon how he had seen her coming from the bank that Friday and how she had told him that she had some shopping she had wanted to do. Then, regardless of what he thought of her manners, but knowing only that while his face was within her hand's distance her fury might yet make her forget what had happened the last time she had hit him, she added, 'I assume you can see yourself out,' and stalked away from him before she did something she would be sorry for.

It took her an absolute age to get to sleep that night. Fuming, she wished she had told Damon Niarkos he could just jolly well ring Sollis Refrigeration again—this time to tell them that he'd made a mistake, and that she was returning.

She was still incredulous when she got up the next morning. The nerve of the man! How *could* he calmly telephone Mr Anderson in England and give in her resignation? How could Mr Anderson have accepted it?

By Wednesday she had started to cool down. It was then she realised that, since she had not yet told Faye and Eugene that she was leaving, maybe to tell them was not now as pressing as it had once been. Oh, she still had the same reason for wanting to leave. God—when she thought of that damned autocrat Damon Niarkos, of his nerve—and—of her love for him... But since, through him, she no longer had a job to go to on Monday, perhaps it would be better to choose her time to tell Faye that she could not stay until after the baby had arrived.

On Thursday Kendra just knew that she would not be catching that plane home tomorrow. As she accepted that, so she accepted that now she had cooled down considerably she was also feeling a shade relieved. Which, she realised, had to make her the most mixed up person she knew. Because love for Damon had made her want to flee—yet that same love for him made her heart sore for a sight of him—and that same love made her relieved that, for a day or so more, perhaps, she could not go.

For all she had not made any concrete arrangements for when she returned to England, though, it had been in her mind to go to Barton Avery this coming weekend. It had been her intention to visit her parents and to call and acquaint Faye's parents with all the best bits about their daughter. But, with things not destined to work out that way, Kendra spent most of Thursday afternoon in writing long letters to her parents, to her aunt and uncle, and to Janice, her flatmate. All the letters contained different pieces of news, but all included the same, 'I'll be home shortly.'

By the time Friday arrived, Kendra was beginning to wonder how she had ever thought she could leave Greece while there was the remotest chance of her staying? The truth was that she had adjusted to Damon's colossal impertinence in giving in her notice for her, and—she faced it squarely—she was yearning with an aching heart for a sight of him. In moments of strength she rehearsed how she would tell Faye and Eugene that night that she was returning to England—as she had said in her letters—shortly. In moments of weakness, however, she felt she would have done anything, and gone to any lengths, just to see Damon.

She went down to dinner that night and felt she had the strength needed, should there be a 'right' moment, to say what she had to say. She entered the sitting-room and her legs suddenly went like jelly the strength she needed gone in moments. For there were three men in the room, but her gaze went straight to Damon. Oh, how she loved him! She turned her head, her mind still full of Damon as she smiled at Eugene and heard him say, 'Damon is joining us for dinner.'

'How—nice,' she replied, and hoped Damon thought that, for politeness' sake, she was lying her head off. Because it wasn't merely nice that he would be with them for the next hour or so, it was wonderful!

Kendra was overwhelmingly aware of Damon when five of them sat down to dinner. Though because her pride would not stand for his receiving so much as a glimmer of a notion of how very much in love with him she was, she was determined that not by unthought word or unthought look would he know it. Remembering the way they had parted, however—not to mention his outrageous nerve in telephoning in her resignation—she thought it would be no surprise to him had she decided never to speak to him again. For the sake of good manners, though, and in the interests of a harmonious dinner-table, she was ready to put all her best efforts into treating him with a surface politeness.

She was eating her way through her first course of some spaghetti-type dish when she became aware that she was not the only one who was putting their best efforts into ensuring that there was no disharmony at the dinner-table. With something of a jolt, her sensitivities suddenly picked up the fact that Eugene, of all people—whose manners were usually impeccable—was having the hardest work not to show that he was displeased about something.

Several minutes later, Kendra took advantage of Medea's coming in to clear away their plates to study Faye's expression. Knowing her cousin as well as she did, it did not take her long to realise that Faye was looking particularly mulish.

Conversation was fairly general during the main course of steak and salad. But Kendra was aware by then that Faye and Eugene must have had a disagreement about something. It was not until Medea had been in again to clear away and to attend to their final course, though, that she gained any idea of what they had quarrelled over.

Opting to finish off with fresh fruit, Kendra was cutting into a shining red apple when Costas, having been talking enthusiastically and at some length about his friend's new sports car, went on, '. . . but we really made her race on the road to Sounion. Well, Zeno did,' he amended quickly, just as if, having forgotten himself in his enthusiasm, he had just realised that he might have earned himself a reprimand from his father for speeding. And, changing the subject fast, he asked his father,

'Weren't you and Faye going to Sounion today? I thought you were taking the day off?'

'It was my idea to take Faye for a short outing as Dr Kostikos prescribed,' Eugene replied, and to Kendra he seemed to be suddenly weighed down with worry. 'But Faye did not want to go, so I went to work.'

'You felt ill, Faye?' Costas asked her gently.

'I...' Faye began, and then, a defiant expression joining her look of stubbornness, she effectively made Kendra stare at her in amazement when she said clearly, 'I hardly think it polite to go out for the day and to leave my cousin on her own. Especially when she has come all this way to keep me company.' Kendra was still staring at her, stupefied, when, placing her serviette down upon the table, Faye said, 'If you'll excuse me, I think I should like to return upstairs.'

She had gone from the room, with Eugene going after her, by the time Kendra had got her breath back from this the first intimation that, because of her, Faye had refused to leave the villa!

'Do you mind if I leave, too?' Costas asked, breaking into Kendra's stunned thoughts. 'I've said I'll go and give Zeno the benefit of my advice,' he added cheerfully.

'Have a good time,' Kendra smiled at him, and it was not until he had gone from the room that she came fully alive to the fact that, with Faye and Eugene gone, and Costas gone, she was left alone with Damon! Oh, grief, she thought, and wanting to flee, wanting to stay, she could see no way of going to her room without first offering him coffee!

She was shying from making the suggestion that they adjourn to the sitting-room, however, when, looking across at her, Damon coolly drawled, 'It would appear, Kendra, that you have become a pawn in your cousin's game to drive her husband demented.'

'A pawn?' Her chin tilted upwards as she took exception not only to what he said, but the way that he said it.

'She has certainly used you as a lever in her refusal to go out with her husband today,' he answered and, unabashed by her haughty stare, he went on, 'Were you not here, she'd have no relative to use, but would have to comply with Eugene's attempts to get her to obey her physician's instructions.'

From the stubborn look which Kendra had witnessed on her cousin's face, she would have said that nothing on God's earth would have Faye doing anything which she did not want to do. But, feeling hurt that clearly Damon would fire a celebratory salvo were she to return to England, Kendra could be stubborn herself. And never was she more determined that he should not know how easy it was for him to wound her.

'That's most unfair!' she told him hostilely. 'Leaving aside the terrible time Faye's having in carrying Eugene's baby, and the fact that Eugene himself expressly asked me to extend my stay, I had every intention of leaving today, and would have gone, too,' she inserted as she paused for breath, 'but for your ensuring that I've no job to go home to! So,' she went storming on, growing more incensed at the injustice she was being served, 'since you're so clever at blaming me, what do you suggest I should do?'

Glaring at him as she flared to an angry end, Kendra wondered what it was about the man, when she had determined at the outset that she would be cool and unruffled, that with a very few words he could make her heated, and outraged. *He*, now, had all the coolness which she had wanted, and was in no way ruffled when, after long moments of studying her irate expression in calm silence, he casually drawled, 'I'm doing nothing tomorrow. For Eugene's sake, I'll take you out for the day.'

Staggered yet again by his cool nerve, Kendra stared at him wide-eyed. Even as she realised that by removing her he would remove any lever Faye had should Eugene attempt to get her out of the villa again tomorrow, Kendra could not get over Damon's sauce. Astounded though she was, however, it did not take her long to give him his answer.

Pushed along by screaming, indignant pride, she denied that weak part of her that would have loved to have spent a whole day in his company, and told him waspishly, 'I'm not surprised you're doing nothing tomorrow. With your charm, I shouldn't bother getting out of bed!' With that, and not caring if he never had another cup of coffee in his life, she slapped her napkin down on the table and marched angrily from the room.

CHAPTER SEVEN

ON REFLECTION, Kendra had realised that, since Eugene must have invited Damon to dine, good manners would see him returning downstairs once Faye was comfortably settled in their suite. But when she awoke the next morning, Kendra was still sufficiently rattled by Damon to care not a jot whether he had been served an after-dinner drink last night or not.

She gathered that Costas must be having a Saturday morning lie-in when she went down to breakfast and he was nowhere to be seen. She was pouring herself a cup of coffee, however, when she heard the sound of male footsteps and looked up, thinking that it was Costas.

'May I join you in a coffee?' Eugene enquired, and sat down at the table with her while, taking up the cup Costas would have used had he been there, she poured him a coffee. Eugene then came to why he had broken with his more usual breakfast-time practice. 'I hope you were not offended by Faye's reference to her being housebound because you are here,' he said, proving to Kendra yet again what a love he was, in that he seemed about to apologise for any offence caused.

'Not at all,' she smiled, but, seeing a way of bringing up the subject of an imminent return to England, 'But it's not very satisfactory, is it?' she said gently. 'I mean, Faye has to get out, but...' Her voice tailed off. 'Perhaps I should...' she went to continue, and took a breath ready to bring out 'go home', but only to find that Eugene thought he had read what she was going to say.

'Perhaps you should come with us?' he suggested.

'Oh, I don't think that's a very good idea,' she said quickly, and hastened to tack on equally quickly, 'I thought...'

'You think Faye and I should get away on our own?' Eugene smiled.

'Er—something like that.'

Eugene pondered for only a moment, and then he went on to reveal, 'I had another outing planned for Faye for today, but I think she will again refuse.'

As he fell silent, so Kendra got the clearest impression that the outing he had planned that day was a rather special one. Realising that she stood to cause a fuss and possibly create more complications rather than ease them if she told Eugene that she would pack and leave at once, Kendra fell to wondering how best she could help.

'I like walking,' she said off the top of her head. 'If you like, I'll take myself off for a long walk. I could...'

But Eugene, although following her drift, was shaking his head. 'I cannot allow you to go out on your own for so many hours,' he immediately scotched the idea.

'But I...' She broke off; Eugene had enough problems without her asserting that she had often taken herself off on a long walk. 'You intend to be out for the whole day?' she enquired slowly, batting away an instant memory of Damon's 'I'm doing nothing tomorrow. For Eugene's sake, I'll take you out for the day'.

'The island where Faye and I spent our honeymoon is not far from here,' Eugene replied. 'It was a blissful time for us, and would please Faye once she was there—I know it would.'

'Ohh,' Kendra breathed on a sigh, and, pushing thoughts of Damon from her head, she asked, 'How about Costas?' remembering that seldom did a day go by that he did not suggest taking her out. 'If he's got nothing else on, he and I could...' Again Eugene's shaking his head made her break off. 'The memory of the last time he took you out is still most fresh in my mind,' Eugene told her. 'Neither Faye nor I would be able to relax, let alone leave home until you were safely back.'

'Oh,' Kendra said, and although she had started to feel that she was going to have to confess to Damon's offer for some minutes now, she was still most reluctant to do so. 'Actually,' she said, and could see that Eugene was waiting for what she had to say. 'Well,' she tried a second reluctant time, 'although I'm sure he will have made other plans by now...' Eugene, the most patient of men, she realised, was still silently waiting, 'Well, actually, D-Damon last night suggested we go somewhere together—today.'

Instantly, Eugene's face was full of smiles. Unlike in the case of Costas, Eugene seemed to have no qualms about her spending the day out somewhere with Damon. Though his smile faded momentarily as he asked, 'But why did you not say that you were going out with him today?'

'Because I'm not. That is to say,' she added quickly as she began to get herself into a tangle, 'I wasn't. I mean—I—er—didn't like to say yes, when he asked me.'

'Ah—you were shy,' Eugene concluded gently, but he was smiling again as he told her happily, 'I will ring Damon now and tell him "yes" for you.'

He was half-way out of the breakfast room before Kendra's sharp 'No!' stopped him.

'You do not like Damon!' he asked, a puzzled look coming to his face.

'It—isn't that,' she replied. 'It's just that—well, he might have gone off the idea this morning.'

'Damon never says anything he doesn't mean.'

'Oh,' said Kendra, and as Eugene waited, it suddenly dawned on her that if she did not do something to help, Faye was going to spend another day housebound. As Kendra saw it then, the whole of whether Eugene and Faye returned to their honeymoon island that day seemed to depend on her—and her pride. Kendra took a shaky breath. 'If—if you'll tell me Damon's number I'll ring him myself,' she told Eugene.

'You would like to go out with Damon?' Eugene thought to ask as he escorted her to his study.

'Yes,' she said; she had fought hard, but everything was against her. 'Yes, I should,' she said, and as she said the words, she knew them to be true.

Eugene was beaming from ear to ear when, having jotted Damon's number down for her, he went off to acquaint his wife with the news that her time of hibernation was over. Kendra guessed that Faye would not be too pleased about it, especially when she realised that she could no longer use their house-guest as a reason for staying home. No doubt she would consider herself betrayed, but Kendra was much more shaky about the phone call she had to make than she was worried about Faye's reactions.

Twice she started to dial, and twice she put the phone back down. In the end it was sheer impatience with herself and the dithering wretch love was making of her which made her dial. Her insides were shaky, but she made herself stay there with the phone glued to her ear until it was answered.

'Kendra Jephcott,' she announced stiffly, and while loving him, she hated him when he said not a word. 'I'm doing nothing today,' his silence made her go on. She hated him some more when, still with not a word, he waited for her continue. 'So,' she said, and took a steadying breath, 'I've decided to allow you to take me out for the day.'

She was ready, at any second, to slam the phone back on its rest. Only by the effort of gripping the phone hard did she prevent herself from doing so. Then, suddenly, she was hearing his reply.

'I'll come for you in an hour,' he drawled. Quietly Kendra put down the phone.

When she left the study she found that she was smiling. Instantly she wiped the smile off her face. She then discovered that she was not at all happy with the dress she had put on that morning.

Nor was she thrilled with anything in her wardrobe when, up in her room, she opted for a fresh-looking dress with short sleeves and a flared skirt. Unsure where Damon would take her, she hoped she was neither under- or over-dressed. She left her room and would by far have preferred to go and wait for Damon without seeing her cousin. But she just couldn't be such a coward.

Because Eugene was home, she did not immediately go in when no one answered her knock, but waited, and knocked again. When no one came, though, Kendra entered the sitting-room and went and knocked on the bedroom door. She was just about to knock again when Faye, a hairbrush in her hand, came and answered it.

'On your own?' Kendra asked pleasantly, observing from Faye's downturned mouth that she was not a bundle of joy that morning.

'Eugene's checking something downstairs,' Faye said shortly, and accused, 'You know, of course, that he's insisting on taking me out?'

'I...' Kendra checked as she wondered if Eugene had said yet where he was taking Faye or if he was intending it to be a surprise. For certain, though, Faye would throw a fit if she thought she was in league with Eugene over this. 'You've got a nice day for it,' she took a middle road.

'A fat lot of help you are!' Faye snapped.

'You've heard that Damon asked me out last night?'

'Much good will it do you,' Faye sniffed, thoroughly out of sorts. 'You've seen for yourself the sort of woman he usually goes out with.'

Kendra wished Faye had not reminded her about Rhodeia Stassinopoulos; the reminder hurt, even if she did manage to stay smiling as she told her, 'Variety is the spice of life—he's not the sort of man I usually go out with either.'

Almost she got a smile out of Faye, but not quite. And Faye was waspish still when she warned, 'Well, don't you believe a lying Greek word he tells you!'

'You *care*?' Kendra grinned as, still hiding her hurt, she refused to give up her attempts to talk Faye out of her sulky mood.

'Oh—go and enjoy yourself!' Faye said reluctantly, and called after her as Kendra went back through the sitting-room and towards the outer door, 'Only consult with me in future *before* you accept the offer of a date!'

'Oh—go and enjoy yourself!' Kendra tossed back teasingly.

She was not in a teasing mood, however, when, opting to go and wait for Damon in the garden, she suffered great wave after wave of jealousy. She remembered the dark-haired, elegant and superbly turned out Rhodeia Stassinopoulos and cringed to think she had imagined for a second that the dress she had opted to wear that day would pass wherever Damon took her.

Kendra stopped cringing when she realised Damon had too much sophistication to either take her anywhere where what she wore mattered, or to let her feel in the least embarrassed about it. She was back to wondering about his relationship with Rhodeia Stassinopoulos, though, and consequently being speared by darts of jealousy, when Costas ambled out to where she was.

'Good morning, Kendra,' he greeted her warmly. 'You're looking more lovely than ever.' He made her day, even if she *was* aware by then that he went in for exaggeration.

'Have you had breakfast?' she asked, for no reason she could think of other than that he must bring out the mother in her.

'Who can eat?' he exclaimed, and sitting down beside her, 'Do you believe in love at first sight?' he asked.

Had he not looked so serious, she might have answered him flippantly. But, because he suddenly seemed so intense and as if he really needed a serious answer, she gave his weighty question some thought. She did not have to think too deeply. Although she had not recognised it for love at the time, she had been affected by Damon from her first moment of meeting him.

But her love was too private to discuss with anyone, so she looked solemnly at Costas, and gently she asked, 'Have you met someone you've fallen instantly in love with?'

He nodded. 'Last night,' he said, his voice hushed as he went on, 'When I called on Zeno, his parents were entertaining some friends. The friends had their daughter, Obelia, with them and, as soon as I saw her, I knew.'

'Oh, Costas,' Kendra said softly, and realised in a moment of empathy with him that the look of fellow feeling he saw in her face caused him to unthinkingly take hold of her hand.

She made no attempt to withdraw it, and did know that fellow feeling when he said, 'When she looked at me and smiled, I felt my heart was going to burst.'

'Have you made arrangements to see her again?' Kendra asked.

'It was difficult, with her parents there,' he replied, and added, 'I think I shall have to have a talk with my father; he will...' Suddenly he broke off, and Kendra followed his eyes, to feel her own heart suddenly start to clamour as though it would burst. For, walking with his usual quiet tread, Damon had come silently up the path.

From the grim look on his face, though, she gathered that he was not well pleased about something. Then she noticed where his eyes were focused, and all at once she knew what that something was. For Costas still had a hold of one of her hands and Damon, having once warned her to leave the son of the house alone, quite plainly did not care for the cosy picture he had just come across. Without a word, he strode past them and into the house.

'Something seems to have upset Damon!' Costas exclaimed, his hold on her hand loosening, and leaving hers altogether as he turned to stare after him. 'Have I forgotten to do something I should have done, I wonder?' he asked.

'Perhaps he's just having a bad day,' Kendra smiled, and only had to mention the name 'Obelia' to have Costas forget any worry he might have about work not done.

She had to own, though, that this time, as Costas spoke quite openly about his love, she was not concentrating so fully as before. She had an idea, from the way Damon had looked when he had gone by just now, that she had just said goodbye to any outing with him.

Wishing with all her heart that she did not give a damn about that, Kendra knew that she *did* give a damn. She wanted her one day with Damon—was it too much to ask, just one day?

'... so if my father happens to know Obelia's father, he can ...' Costas was saying when they saw Damon, looking only marginally less grim than he had before, coming from the house.

'If you're ready...' Damon clipped to her as soon as he neared them.

'Where are you going?' Costas wanted to know.

Kendra, at that point, ceased to wonder at the crazy, mixed-up person she had been since she had known Damon. Because while her heart lifted that she was, after all, going to have her day with him, she was at one and the same time extremely annoyed with him when, not bothering to hide the pleasure he felt at having nipped anything she had going with Costas in the bud, he replied, 'I'm taking Kendra out—for the day.'

'You'll have to wait while I get my bag,' she said shortly, and left them to go indoors and to wonder yet again at this love business which had her both wanting to hit Damon for being such a swine seemingly without effort, yet not wanting to deprive herself of his company.

Collecting her bag, she stayed in her room long enough to check her appearance. Damon had been wearing casual shirt and trousers, she remembered, and—a smile started to curve her mouth—her dress was just right.

She had run lightly down the stairs and was just crossing the hall when she saw Eugene approaching the stairs from the direction of his study.

'Enjoy your island,' she called happily.

'Enjoy—wherever you're going,' he smiled.

Kendra wiped all signs of inner happiness from her as she went out into the sunlight. But, because she thought she should make some effort or the atmosphere between her and Damon was just going to go from bad to worse—

she just knew it—she said brightly, 'Back in two shakes of a lamb's tail.'

Costas burst out laughing at this quaint English expression, and Damon said, 'I'm sure,' and went with her down the garden path.

The first half-hour of their journey passed with nothing very much being said. Then, still intent on keeping the atmosphere light, Kendra thought that some conversation was called for.

'I hope you didn't mind me telephoning you this morning,' she said nicely. No reply! 'Only Eugene told me this morning that he wanted to take Faye back to their honeymoon island and . . .' Her voice petered out. With Damon not chipping in with any word, suddenly her conversation with Eugene seemed dreadfully complicated to explain.

After a second or two of her unfinished sentence, though, Damon did have something to chip in with. And Kendra's heart lifted yet again, because, just as though he had decided some effort was needed on his part too if the atmosphere between them was not to deteriorate, his voice was quite pleasant as he said, 'So Eugene told me.'

'He told . . . Eugene rang you before I did?' she asked in surprise.

But Damon was shaking his head and, watching him from a close distance, Kendra could have sworn that there was a smile teasing around the corners of his mouth when he replied, 'I had a few words with him before we left.'

'Ah,' Kendra murmured, and all at once she was starting to feel as sunny as the day, because the further on they drove, the more Damon seemed to lose that hint of aggressiveness which he usually reserved for her.

Indeed, she was sure it was not her imagination but that a touch of warmth was entering his tones as she began to ask him questions about his country. She was positive that warmth and a friendliness had crept in when, passing an olive grove, she asked questions about green and black olives. Some olives were picked by hand while they were still green, he told her, while others were left to ripen. Nets were then laid on the ground and, when the rest of the olives were ripe, the trees were shaken and the black olives would fall to the ground.

Happy within herself, being with Damon feeling—so right—Kendra gave herself up to enjoying the splendid panoramic views as, while keeping more or less to the rugged coastline, they travelled amid gigantic mountains until they approached the Corinth Canal.

The Corinth Canal separated the Peloponnese from mainland Greece, Damon had told her. 'Can we...could we stop and take a look?' she asked tentatively.

'I knew you were going to ask that,' he said, and there was definitely a smile around his mouth when, as if not at all put out that she had an enquiring mind, he added, 'Which is why we'll stop once we've crossed over the canal bridge.'

Kendra's heart was positively singing when, with Damon beside her, she stood on a footbridge and stared in wonder at the canal below, at what, in the latter end of the last century, had been achieved by man. It was no wonder to her that the sheer sides, sliced out of rock and going down an incredible depth, had taken twelve years to excavate. Her only wonder was that, given the tools of the day, it had not taken longer.

She was grateful to Damon that he appeared in no hurry and allowed her to look her fill. 'Seen enough?' he enquired when she turned away from the great feat of engineering.

'I still can't believe it,' she said as they walked back to the car. 'I shall just have to come and take another look one day.'

From there, Damon drove her to view the site of ancient Corinth, and pointed out the spot where St Paul was said to have appeared to defend himself and the Christian religion.

'And now,' Damon smiled when, her imagination fired, she had walked among the ruins of the old market place, 'I must feed you, or risk your collapse.'

Again Kendra smiled; she just could not help it. By then, she was growing more and more confident that nothing could mar what the gods had decided would be her special day.

She was, therefore, wishing to bite her tongue off when, opting to eat in the gardens of a smart hotel which Damon had found, she should feel that she had ruined the friendly atmosphere by thoughtlessly referring to her cousin and her husband.

'I wonder if Faye and Eugene have made it to their island,' she mused out loud, more, she realised, because, happy herself, she wanted everyone else to be happy.

'You've done what you could in that respect,' Damon said, and to Kendra he seemed so off-hand that she suddenly had the most awful feeling that, far from enjoying himself as she had so sunnily believed, he was finding the day hard going.

'Perhaps I should have done more—and taken myself off back to England,' she retorted shortly and, not wanting him to see the hurt in her eyes, she looked down at her plate and to the *garithes pilafi* she had ordered, but no longer wanted.

'You seem anxious to get back to England!' All sign of friendliness had gone from his voice, though Kendra had hardly expected any other—not now. 'Perhaps you should go back,' he said to wound her further. 'Perhaps, too, you should telephone your "friend" Nigel to meet you, the same way that he came to the airport to see you go!'

At that, Kendra's head shot up. Startled, she stared at him, because she could only ever recall mentioning Nigel's name once. That had been on the way back from the Acropolis when Damon had thought Nigel her lover. But that Damon still remembered his name caused her heart to misbehave, because, incredibly, it had sounded every bit as if he was—jealous! Her heart soon steadied down to a dull beat, though, when she saw him looking at her with nothing but aloofness in his dark eyes. Jealous he definitely was not. Anti Kendra Jephcott he most definitely was.

Damn him, and his mammoth memory for names, she thought, and damn Nigel too. It would not have taken much for her to have got up and left the table and chanced her luck in getting back to Athens some way or another. With a tremendous effort, though, she rose over her hurt that Damon seemed to want her to return to England and, although she could do nothing about her cool tone, her voice was even when she replied to his sharp comments.

'For your information, I will return to England shortly. For your further information, I shall not be telephoning Nigel, because I've decided not to see him again.'

She had no idea why she had told him that last bit. It was a fact that she had barely given Nigel a thought since she had come to Greece, and another fact that Damon could not be in the least interested. She was keeping her attention strictly on the prawns and olives on the plate in front of her, however, when, his voice as even as hers had been, Damon remarked, 'I hardly think that saying goodbye to Costas, and ending your romance with your English beau, will leave you without admirers.'

Glancing up, Kendra saw that the aloof look had gone from his eyes, and suddenly all the ice that was building up inside her against him started to melt.

'What about *your* admirers?' she questioned.

'You?' he enquired.

She laughed, half in jest, half so he should not know he had hit on the truth, and that she more than admired him. She shook her head and, deserving an Oscar for her display of non-jealousy, she murmured, 'I don't know of all your lady-friends, of course, but I was once introduced to a Miss Rhodeia Stassinopoulos.'

'Hm, Rhodeia,' he said, and all at once Kendra's day was lovely again, for not only was there a hint of a smile on his face, but his words were pure magic to her, when he revealed, 'Weeks ago my sister Astrea asked me to ensure that her friend Rhodeia would not spend a lonely evening in her hotel during her forthcoming two-day business trip to Athens.'

'Rhodeia is more your sister's friend than yours, then?' Kendra queried, trying to sound only as curious as she should sound and not in any way as relieved as she did feel.

'Did I not say at the time?' Damon enquired.

Kendra was by then of the opinion that there was not a word said or unsaid by him that Damon could not remember without having to enquire about it, but she replied, 'I don't believe you did,' and gave herself up to enjoying his company.

As far as she could tell, she thought he was beginning to enjoy her company too. For, as they lingered over coffee, his good humour appeared restored, and the small hiccup in the day looked forgotten.

From then on, her time with him, her precious time with him, seemed to flash by. She feared as they left their eating place that Damon might consider his day's work done and return to Athens. But, to her enormous delight, as if to prove that he was enjoying her company, Damon returned to the road they had been travelling on, the one that led away from Athens.

He drove confidently and well, and, knowing that she would be taking out this day and savouring it long, long after it had gone, Kendra hoarded up memory after memory as the car sped along. She stored up so many pictures. Pictures of how, seemingly miles away from civilisation, beehives had been placed so that in due time someone could come along and collect wild bee honey. Pictures of netting on rocky mountains, the netting presumably there to prevent rock-fall damage. Pictures of hibiscus, of orange trees and of wild bamboo that lined their route. But, most of all, she was overwhelmingly conscious the whole time of the man by her side—the man she was in love with.

The next time Damon stopped the car, they were at a place called Epidaurus. 'There's a restored ancient theatre here which is known for its unique acoustics,' Damon smiled, and came round and assisted her out of the car. 'I thought you might care to see it.'

They had to walk some small way before they came to the site of the open-air theatre. But in Damon's company, Kendra would not have cared had it been miles and miles.

'It's awe-inspiring!' she exclaimed when, as they reached the ancient site, her attention became riveted on the semi-circle of tier after tier of stone seats. Her attention switched to become riveted on what Damon was saying while he detailed that the theatre could seat an audience of fourteen thousand and how every summer during the Epidaurus Festival ancient tragedies and other events were performed there.

Again he seemed in no hurry, but appeared content to let her look her fill. Wanting to savour every moment, Kendra felt that she never wanted to leave Epidaurus, or Greece, or Damon. But common sense had a nasty habit of making itself known, and at last she looked away from the scene.

'Dusk will have fallen if I stay here much longer,' she said on a gulped breath as she turned to find that Damon had been watching her. She smiled, but he did not return her smile, and suddenly pride had ferreted out a perversity in her nature which pushed her to say, 'I expect you'll want to get back to Athens before it gets dark.'

'I doubt we should make it before dark even if we left now,' Damon told her. 'But what makes you think I want to get back to Athens?' he asked, and suddenly he was smiling.

Kendra's whole world was all at once much brighter. 'Just a thought,' she said, and could not hold down a smile of her own. She saw Damon's eyes on her mouth as her smile parted her lips, and she knew, positively knew, that he was going to kiss her.

But the suspense was too great to bear and, as his head started to come nearer, she closed her eyes. A moment later, she just had to open them again. And she was glad that she did so, because Damon had turned his head from her and it was clear that he had no intention whatsoever of kissing her, and that her highly active imagination had a lot to answer for.

Her heart, none the less, was beating erratically when, in a perfectly natural voice, Damon commented, 'I thought I'd show you some more of the scenery—while the light holds. We can perhaps stop around nine and have dinner. Does that meet with your approval?' he asked, his voice friendly.

'That would be—er—very nice,' Kendra said politely.

In the next few hours, she fell more and more under the spell of Damon. They were still following a coast road, yet with huge towering mountains to be seen everywhere, and she savoured every moment. Darkness had fallen several hours since when he pulled up at an hotel and escorted her inside.

'You're sure about the *kaccavia*?' Damon asked, having guided her over the menu. She looked across at him and her heart gave a breathless lurch. Because she was certain that it was not her imagination now, but that there was definitely admiration in his dark eyes as he looked back at her.

'I—er—insist on having it,' she said huskily, as she tried hard to remember what only a moment ago he had told her about the soup she had just ordered. If memory served, *kaccavia* was a famous fish soup which derived its name from the earthenware pot in which it was cooked.

'Then I, too, will have *kaccavia*,' he smiled, and suddenly Kendra was swamped by his charm.

What time it was when they left the restaurant and began their journey back to Athens, Kendra neither knew nor cared. Because on that drive a companionable silence fell between them, and, praying that it was not her imagination, she had the wonderful feeling that Damon liked her.

'Tired?' he asked as they drew yet closer to Athens.

'Not a bit,' she replied, determined regardless of the hour that she was not going to miss a moment of this, her day with Damon, by nodding off. 'I've really enjoyed today,' she went on to tell him, but halted there, afraid that he might glean that he was the sole reason for that. 'There have been so many new sights to see, so many new impressions, so many...' Her voice tailed off, it seeming to her that she was in danger of going over the top, whatever she said.

But—making her fall even more in love with him—Damon did not appear to think that she was going the least little bit over the top, and his charm swamped her again when, with a smile in his voice, he told her, 'I, too, have really enjoyed today.' And if that wasn't enough for her to be going on with, 'But who says the day is over?'

'It—um...' must be midnight, she so nearly said; only in time did she check herself and make it a question by saying, '...isn't?'

'It's Saturday still, the night of the week when most people are later going to bed, would you not agree?' he asked.

'Oh, yes,' she agreed happily, and stayed silent while she wondered, since he had suggested that the day wasn't yet over, what he had in mind to do now.

'Despite your refusal to admit to tiredness, I think that perhaps you are maybe a little tired,' he commented, that smile that charmed her so still in his voice. 'For that reason, and since from this direction we have to more or less pass my home before we reach the home of Eugene, I should like to welcome you to my home for a drink to close our day.'

Kendra's heart lifted at the pure and utter thrill it was to know that Damon *must* like her, because no way otherwise would he so much as consider welcoming her into his home.

'That sounds very nice,' she told him, cringing at her use of the insipid word 'nice' when to her it was more 'absolutely fantastic' than 'nice'. She loved him, and she thought he liked her—and he was taking her to see his home, where they would have a drink to close their day.

'Please—come in,' Damon smiled as, leaving his car parked on the forecourt of an impressive-looking villa, he escorted her to the front door and unlocked it.

Feeling slightly bemused by then, Kendra stepped over his threshold into ankle-deep carpet, and could not deny a glow of excitement as he touched his hand to her elbow, and guided her to his drawing-room.

'Sit here,' he said easily, and piloted her to a plush, well-padded easy chair. 'Now, what would you like to drink?'

In actual fact, it was enough for Kendra just to be in his home, but since the whole reason for her being there was to close the day with some sort of a nightcap, 'I'll have a small brandy, if I may,' she accepted quietly, and while he went to get her drink, her eyes photographed the room so that she could remember it later and imagine him there.

The walls were a cool white, the carpet a plain pale green. The curtains were a darker shade of green velvet. Other chairs in the large room were as well padded as the one she was occupying, as were a couple of couches the room housed. Kendra's gaze was on the paintings on the walls when Damon came and, standing in front of her, handed her the brandy she had asked for.

As things turned out, though, she never got to taste her brandy. Because as her hand went up to take it from him, so with horrified eyes she spotted that the way his nearness affected her had manifested itself in the visible trembling of her outstretched hand. The impulse to hide what he could do to her beat the intelligence which would have warned of an accident. For, without pausing to think, Kendra pulled back her hand to hide it, just as Damon was about to deliver the glass into her safekeeping. The result was that, with the quickest reactions in the world, he could not prevent some of the brandy from tipping on to her.

In the few seconds that followed Damon's stepping back as she shot to her feet rather than christen his furniture with brandy, Kendra knew complete confusion.

'I'm a clown!' she wailed as, recapturing his hold on the glass with one hand, with his other he offered her his handkerchief to mop herself up.

'You're—beautiful,' he smiled softly, and, as Kendra ceased mopping-up operations to stare at him in breathless suspense of the moment, 'You really are,' he said.

'Do—you think so?' she asked, and with her heart beating wildly as she stared at him saucer-eyed, she just was not thinking at all.

'I've always thought so,' Damon confessed quietly, and, taking the handkerchief from her, he put it, along with the brandy-glass, down on a nearby table. Unhurriedly then, he gently took her into his arms. 'From the moment I first saw you, I thought you were beautiful,' he charmed her some more, and the next thing Kendra knew was that his mouth was meeting her eager waiting lips.

'Oh, Damon,' she murmured his name when, breaking that tender kiss, he looked deeply into her emotion-filled eyes.

'You don't object that I cannot control my need to have you in my arms?' he asked, and, made speechless by his words, all Kendra could do was silently shake her head. Then his mouth was over hers again.

As she delighted in the thrill of being this close to him, her arms went up and around him. And, as Damon moved her gently yet more closely to him, Kendra moved her feet those few small inches forward until their bodies were in yet closer contact.

'Beautiful Kendra!' he breathed when next their mouths parted, and he gazed deeply into her shining, acquiescent green eyes.

Again he kissed her; this time, though, something else had entered his kisses—something different. This time, although there was still a gentleness in his lovemaking, Kendra was left in no doubt that Damon was the one in charge of what happened from then on. She felt his hands warm at her back, and then they caressed to her shoulders and down her arms. And she was glad that he was the one in charge, because she was in a land of passion such as she had never been in, and she felt incapable of coherent thought.

She moaned softly when his mouth left hers and he trailed kisses down her throat to the V-neck of her dress. 'Will you be mine, Kendra?' he asked, and as his hands moved to the back of her again, and he pressed her to him, she wanted to tell him yes, yes, yes. Which made it most odd, when she could deny him nothing, that she should hesitate.

'I...' she said chokily, and, wanting him with all her being, she was glad that he was not put off that she seemed to be demurring, but had put his own interpretation on the reason for it.

'It will be all right for you to stay here,' he misunderstood her hesitation. 'Eugene and Faye are spending the night on their island, and will not be home to worry about you not being there.'

'Oh,' Kendra breathed, and, only half taking in what he was saying, she went on to as good as remove all barriers when she added, 'Th-that's—all right, then.'

In the next moment, Damon's mouth was over hers, teasing her lips apart. Her heart fluttered wildly when she felt his fingers busy at the bodice of her dress, and when the backs of those warm fingers smoothed over the swell of her breasts Kendra ached for him.

He had one arm around her, and had transferred his other hand to the side of her face, when he whispered, 'Come with me, sweet love.'

Kendra had barely any sensation or knowledge that she had walked with him from his drawing-room until, half-way up the stairs with him, she suddenly halted. Suddenly she realised that they must be on the way to his bedroom.

'Something wrong?' he queried as she hung back.

Looking at him, Kendra saw the flame of smouldering desire burning in the eyes that looked back at her. For all that, however, he made no move to force her upwards, but waited for her to tell him if indeed, there was something wrong.

'Not a thing,' Kendra overcame her nerves to tell him. She even smiled gently when, wanting this time of oneness with him, she began to ascend the stairs again.

Inside his room, where the large bed seemed to her just then to dominate the whole of it, she had another moment of nerves. Impatient with herself, though, it was she who began the next passionate interlude when she put her arms around Damon and pressed her body close up against him.

A low moan left him, and she felt exultant, and the next moment, Damon had taken over. 'Sweet, sweet love,' he breathed, and suddenly his experienced fingers were at the fastenings of her clothes.

In next to no time those experienced fingers had removed her dress. As Kendra felt the heat of his body against her so, with the colour hot in her face, she realised, absolutely staggered, that most of her underclothing had been removed from her too. More, as Damon stood with her in one single undergarment, so she discovered that all she had on were her briefs! In a state of shock, nerves and wanting, she also realised at that moment that beside such experience she was going to show up as very inexperienced.

It seemed only right to her then—and as Damon began to urge her towards that large bed she accepted that she was not thinking very clearly—that she should make her excuses in advance.

'D-Damon,' she said, and gave a choking cough when, looking at him, she could not mistake the fire that burned there in his eyes.

'Kendra,' he teased softly, the teasing way he said her name making it easier for her without his knowing it.

'Kiss me—and forgive me,' she said simply.

His answer was to pull her once more up against his broad chest, and gently, as her breasts moved on his skin and his hands caressed down inside the back of her briefs, he kissed her. 'So I've kissed you,' he said, his voice thick in his throat as, with his hands on the pert mounds of her rear, he pulled her to him. 'Now what have I to forgive you for?' he asked, and added, when she delayed too long, 'If you would please tell me quickly. I confess, I cannot wait much longer to feel your beautiful body naked with mine on that bed.'

'I—d-don't want you to be disappointed,' Kendra found her voice to tell him.

'Disappointed?' he queried, making her breath catch as he moved his hands, one to caress to her hip, the other to her breast.

'I—haven't very much—experience,' she whispered.

'You're doing all right so far,' he smiled. Then, as his head came down once more and it seemed that he was about to claim his lips with his, suddenly he stilled. Suddenly he pulled back. All at once his hands ceased to caress her and, every bit as if he was remembering the way she had hung back on the stairs, in a voice that had gone oddly quiet, he asked tautly, 'How much experience do you have?'

Afterwards she realised that she should have guessed from his quiet tone that things could go very much amiss. But just then all that she wanted was that he should know in advance the way it might be.

'Well—none at all, really,' she told him. 'That is,' she went on, not quite understanding the look of shocked disbelief that was coming to his eyes, 'I've been kissed, a good few times before, but...' She broke off to take a shaky breath. 'But this is the first time I've—er—been near a man's bed,' she confessed.

Instantly she felt cold. The moment Damon's hands abruptly left her, she felt bereft. But as soon as he stepped back to put a yard or so of daylight between them, she felt not only cold and bereft but awkward too.

'Theos!' he exclaimed, and she was not sure that he had not lost some of his colour. 'Are you telling me that you're a *virgin*!'

Kendra guessed that actions must have spoken louder than words because, as some small measure of desire started to leave her and she self-consciously brought her arms over to cover her naked breasts, she saw Damon's jaw drop incredulously. And, even as she was saying, 'I'm sorry, but—y-yes,' she was amazed by the instant change that came over him.

'You—you...' he started to grate and, as if totally stuck for words, *'Theos!'* he exploded, and to her utter astonishment, as if needing some action, some control, he bent to pick up his clothes. He had the control he wanted when he straightened, when, in a voice that cut like a whiplash, he thundered, 'Get dressed! Join me downstairs!'

Kendra was too paralysed with astonishment to move when, without a backward look, Damon strode to the door, opened it, and strode out.

CHAPTER EIGHT

FOR perhaps two minutes Kendra just stood, dumb-struck, and stared at the door which Damon had gone through. But, as it dawned on her that, quite plainly, Damon had gone off the idea of wanting her body naked with his on that bed, so she awoke from her frozen immobility.

The word 'naked' brought her to an awareness of her own lack of clothing, and like some over-reactivated automaton she speedily did something to remedy that situation.

Having got into her clothes with lightning speed, however, she took another five minutes to gather up the courage to go downstairs and face Damon again. As yet, she felt too stunned, too confused by all that had happened, and by the swiftness of events, to be able to think with any objectivity about any of it.

She eventually left Damon's bedroom having realised that, with her emotions in such upheaval, objective thinking stood not a chance.

She was shaking like a leaf when, from the top of the stairs, she saw Damon pacing about like come caged animal as he waited, impatiently, for her to appear.

He glanced up as though he had heard her, and as scarlet flooded her face she saw from his grim expression that it was as if their lovemaking had never taken place. Had he smiled, she might have smiled back—she didn't know for sure, she was still very much confused. But when, as though she had got it completely wrong, and he did not like her so much as a tiny bit, he scowled as she stepped from the last stair-tread into the hall, Kendra's pride took charge.

'Are you—all right?' he grunted, his eyes on where her receding colour had left her pale.

'Never better!' she retorted coolly, and, not waiting for him to escort her to the door, she did not pause in her stride, but went straight for it.

Not another word passed between them on the car ride to her cousin's home. What Damon was thinking Kendra neither knew nor cared. Some of her numbness was wearing off, and she had enough to cope with in holding weak tears at bay.

As she anticipated, his courtesy held to the extent that when they reached Eugene's villa, Damon got out of the car and escorted her up the garden path. He did not, as he had before, escort her inside the house, but, seeing one of the maids cross in front of a downstairs window, he said harshly, 'Sybil has waited up for you,' and without another word he turned about and left her.

Damon's earlier words came back to haunt her as Kendra walked stiff-backed the rest of the way up the path. Remembering how he had more or less said that, with Faye and Eugene spending the night on their island, it would be quite all right for her to spend the night with him, suddenly anger started to nip. He had deliberately set out to seduce her! It hadn't meant a thing to him! She was no more to him than—than Eugene's servant, Sybil, Kendra suddenly and painfully realised.

He hadn't cared a damn that Sybil might well have waited up the whole night for her to come home, she fumed as she entered the villa. Just as he didn't care a damn that... Her thoughts broke off when, having apparently heard her come in, Costas suddenly appeared from the sitting-room.

'Costas!' Kendra exclaimed, and suddenly felt dreadful that it seemed everyone in residence had waited up for her. 'I . . .' she began as a prelude to her apology, when all at once she sensed that something awful was wrong. 'What's happened?' she asked quickly.

'Faye's in a nursing home,' Costas took the breath from her body by telling her, and as he guided her from the hall and into the sitting-room, Kendra discovered that Sybil was not up on account of her. Apparently she had been up making coffee for Costas on his return from a stressful time at the nursing home. Faye, it seemed, had been in danger of losing her baby.

'Oh, the poor love,' Kendra whispered. 'How are things now?'

'They're still not too good, which is why they're keeping her there.'

Kendra's heart went out to her, and as she thought of Eugene, her heart went out to him too. 'How's your father?' she asked Costas.

'As you can imagine, blaming Dr Kostikos for daring to say that Faye must have some time away from the house, and blaming himself that he listened to him for a second.'

A short while later, a cup of coffee in front of her too, Kendra had learned that her cousin and Eugene had been on their island when things had begun to go wrong for Faye. Eugene had wasted no time in getting medical help, but, beside himself with anguish, he had left Faye only when the medical team had ejected him from her room. That was when he had telephoned Costas. Costas had gone to him at once. Eugene had refused to leave the nursing home that night.

Wanting to help in any way she could, Kendra began, 'Do you think I should go to the nursing home . . .' but

Costas, suddenly seeming to be much more grown up, interrupted her.

'She's in the best of hands, Kendra,' he told her quietly, and added, 'I'll take you to see her tomorrow...' he broke off to take a look at his watch '...today,' he amended, and thought to ask, 'Did you enjoy your outing with Damon?'

'Very much,' she replied, and tacked on as if it was by the way, 'He decided not to come in because of the lateness of the hour.'

There were not many hours of the night left when Kendra climbed into bed, for which she was truly thankful because, unable to sleep, she found the hours of darkness a mental nightmare. When she was not worrying about Faye and what she must be suffering, and being anxious about Eugene and what he must be suffering, Kendra was suffering an anguish of her own.

Even while she still loved Damon Niarkos, she damned him to hell. Again she became convinced that he had calculatingly set out to seduce her, but that what he had not taken into his calculations was that she was a virgin. She had his Greek honour to thank that that was still the case, she supposed, but when she thought of how they had only gone out together for the sake of Eugene's getting Faye out of the house, Kendra damned Damon some more. He knew full well before they set off that Eugene planned to stay on that island overnight. He had decided, in advance, that, since there was no urgent reason to bring her back to her cousin's home, he might as well have some return for having put himself out that day.

Kendra hurriedly left her bed when at dawn it came to her that for Damon to think she would put up no objections to going to bed with him might mean that he had realised she was in love with him!

Going cold at the very thought, Kendra hurried with her ablutions and wished she need never see him again. She was still squirming with mortification that Damon might have seen her love for him when she went down to breakfast.

It was a surprise to her to see Costas already down on a Sunday morning, but seeing him took thoughts of Damon out of her head for a while. 'You've heard how Faye is?' she enquired quickly, her sixth sense telling her that he had left his bed early to telephone the nursing home.

'Things are improved,' he told her. 'Faye still has her baby, and the emergency is over.' At which good news he took a drink of thick, black coffee.

They chatted about Faye for a few minutes, then Kendra asked, 'When can she come home?'

'Not for a day or two,' he replied. 'I spoke with my father over the phone, and he said that because they want her to stay quiet, they want to keep her with them for a few days more.'

'She's allowed visitors, though?' Kendra asked.

'Of course,' Costas smiled. 'I've arranged with my father that you and I will go this afternoon. You will like that?' he asked.

'Yes, please,' she accepted.

She spent a lazy morning, mainly by the pool, and was glad of Costas's company. For he had a few problems of his own, and he discussed his love Obelia at great length, giving Kendra small chance to dwell on her love for Damon. Apparently, Costas had not yet had a chance to ask his father if he knew Obelia's father, and with Eugene being so distracted just now over Faye, he did not think that now was the right time to talk to him on the matter. And, in love, Costas was having a terribly hard time in being patient.

Without actually thinking about it, Kendra had assumed that the next time she would see Eugene would be when she and Costas went visiting that afternoon. She was therefore most surprised when at lunch time she saw him standing in the dining-room talking to Costas.

'You didn't expect to see me, I can tell,' he greeted her, and as Kendra took in how tired he looked and as though he had not slept in an age, 'It seemed to me, now that things are more settled with Faye, that I should return home to bathe and have a change of clothes.'

'How was Faye when you left?' Kendra asked.

'More contented within herself, but wanting very much to come home,' Eugene replied solemnly.

Most of the meal time passed with the conversation mainly on Faye and the fright she had given Eugene when he had feared not only for the baby's life but, more particularly—and possibly over-reacting—for the life of his beloved wife.

He was, however, very anxious to get back to her, and even if her condition was now stable and no longer giving cause for concern, the meal was no sooner over than he was suggesting that they make for the nursing home.

'Did you phone Damon, as I asked?' he queried of Costas on the way from the dining-room.

'I tried, several times,' Costas told him, and grinned as he added, 'but he must have some heavy date today—he's been out each time I rang.'

Because Eugene intended to remain at the nursing home for as long as he could, he suggested that they take two cars so that Kendra and Costas would not be stuck for transport home.

'Kendra will come with me,' Eugene told his son as they went out to the cars.

At any other time Kendra might have thought it amusing that when Eugene set off at a sedate pace, the sports car enthusiast Costas, rather than incur his parent's wrath at this particular time, was having to content himself to drive sedately behind. But she was not thinking of Costas just then; her head was too busy with remembering how Faye had warned her not to believe a lying word Damon said. Her jealousy reached a peak when, ignoring the fact that Faye had been feeling a trifle hostile towards her at the time, Kendra was more inclined to believe that he had been lying his Greek head off when he had said that Rhodeia was his sister's friend. She'd like to bet he didn't even have a sister—by the name of Astrea or any other.

Thinking of the knowing way in which Costas had said Damon must have a heavy date that day, her jealousy reached an even higher peak. If his date for the day was not Rhodeia Stassinopoulos, then she was darned sure that he would be occupied with someone equally stunning. Kendra sighed unhappily as, thinking of how she had barely slept last night, she realised that it was certain that Damon Niarkos had not lost so much as a wink of sleep over her last night.

'That was a big sigh!' Eugene commented as he pulled into the parking area outside a large, square-looking building. And, unwittingly making her feel guilty, he misread the reason for her sigh, and added, 'Do not worry, Kendra; Faye, I have been doubly assured, is in no danger.'

He was impatient by then, though, to be with his wife again, and, not waiting for Costas, who seemed to be having a small problem finding a parking spot, Eugene took Kendra with him into the nursing home.

Making a beeline for his wife's room, he stopped at one of the doors and opened it and then stood back for Kendra to go in first. Knowing instinctively that he did not want to wait even that split second, and that he wanted to be the first to greet Faye, Kendra stepped quickly to one side. Whereupon Eugene wasted no time. Following him in, though, Kendra was halted by the way Faye held her arms out to her husband, and clung tearfully on to him. The way in which Eugene clung on to his wife, too, was enough to have Kendra quickly ducking out of the room.

Feeling slightly stunned, she stood by a wall in the corridor and realised, if she never realised anything else, that Faye was very much in love with her husband!

Remembering the way they had clung to each other just now, and, from what she had seen, were more than likely still clinging to each other, Kendra felt it would be an intrusion to go in just yet.

Which was how she came to be still in the corridor when a few minutes later Costas came around the corner. 'Have they thrown you out?' he teased.

She shook her head and, smiling, she allowed him to think that she had waited there for him in case he had not known which room was his stepmother's.

Faye was all smiles when they went in, and so, too, was Eugene. The four of them chatted away for some while until Eugene said he thought he would go and have another word with the doctor, and Costas begged to be excused as he was 'dying for the need of a cigarette'.

Left alone with her cousin, Kendra commiserated with her some more. 'I'm so sorry about the awful time you've had,' she told her gently.

'And I'm sorry I was bitchy to you yesterday,' Faye apologised.

'Crikey—you remember your few cross-patch words after all that's happened to you since then!' exclaimed Kendra on a laugh.

But Faye was not laughing when she quietly agreed, 'A lot had happened since yesterday.'

And Kendra just knew that her cousin was not speaking solely about the baby she was expecting. Quite without thinking, she said, 'You've realised you're in love with Eugene.'

'I realised that a long while ago,' Faye replied. 'And that,' she added, 'was when everything went haywire, for me.'

'Because...' Kendra began, but could not go on. Now that Faye was in love with Eugene, it somehow seemed sordid to speak of how she had married him for his bank balance.

Faye, however, had no such qualms about bringing it all out in the open. 'Because I'd married him for his money,' she said that which Kendra could not say. 'There was I, newly married, newly pregnant, and suddenly, I was totally stunned to wake up one morning to discover that where he went was where I wanted to go and that if tomorrow he suddenly went broke, then I wouldn't give a damn as long as he was all right. That, in fact, I was in love with him.'

'Ohh!' Kendra sighed, feeling a shade misty-eyed. She cleared a constriction in her throat, and then she just had to ask, 'But where was the problem—you must know that Eugene positively adores you. Why, he...'

'I know, I know,' Faye cut her off, smiling. 'Blame it on my hormones being all out of balance with the baby or something, because, being in love for the first time in my life, for the first time in my life I became totally unsure of myself. As a consequence I've acted completely differently from the way I've wanted to act. As I saw it then, how could any man love me when I was so fat and ugly? I was convinced Eugene was only looking after me because he wanted the child—and not me at all.'

'Oh, love,' Kendra sympathised, realising the mental agony which Faye had been through. But she smiled a teasing smile as she questioned that which she already knew the answer to. 'Eugene has been able to convince you otherwise, I take it.'

It was Faye's turn to look misty-eyed. 'My poor darling, he was absolutely distraught when he thought I might die. I'd been sedated, but I was still conscious when I overheard him actually threatening the doctor "Forget the baby—save my wife. Let anything happen to her and I'll personally see that something happens to you!"'

'Good grief, Faye!' Kendra exclaimed aghast.

'Exactly,' Faye commented. 'What woman in her right mind wouldn't refuse to die—not that I was anywhere near it—after hearing her love say something like that?'

'I'm so glad for you,' Kendra told her warmly.

'So am I,' Faye grinned. 'Oh, you just can't know how glad I am to feel good about myself again. All Eugene's doing, of course.' She was still grinning when she said, 'In fact, I feel so good about absolutely everything that I might even write a letter to my father and apologise for calling him a miserable old bastard.'

'Faye—you didn't!' Kendra exclaimed.

'I did,' Faye laughed, and was unrepentant when she said, 'It's his fault, he shouldn't be so narrow-minded.'

'Er—nobody's perfect,' Kendra murmured, but she had to laugh too.

Shortly afterwards Costas returned, but, although Faye beamed a smile at Eugene when he came back, her smiles and laughter soon departed when, in answer to her urgent question of, 'Did he say I can come home?' Eugene shook his head.

'Not yet,' he told her gently, and as her face fell, he sat of the side of her bed and took her in his arms. Kendra read it as a signal for her and Costas to leave.

They went out to the car with neither Faye nor Eugene seeming to be aware that they had left. 'Where would you like to go now?' Costas asked.

'Home,' Kendra replied, and as he drove her to his home, she knew that the time had come for her to go home, to England.

She spent the time until dinner trying to find one single, solitary reason why she should remain, but there was not one. Eugene had invited her to stay because he was so concerned about Faye. He had not known it, but he had been the key to what was bothering her. Faye had doubted that, 'fat and ugly', he could truly love her, and had thought him more concerned about the baby than her. But, having seen Faye and Eugene wrapped in each other's arms today, with Faye now confident of his love, Kendra could not see that her help was needed.

She dined with Costas and, when he asked her after the meal was over if she would like to go for a drive, she told him that she had a few things she wanted to do in her room.

'Would you mind, then, if I left you on your own while I drove over to see my friend Zeno?' he asked after a few seconds of thought.

'Of course not,' she smiled, and returned to her room, realising that nothing seemed to have any appeal any more and trying to drum up hate against Damon that it was all his fault.

Having decided in her hate session against him that he was a lying, seducing rat, who probably had stunning beauties like Rhodeia Stassinopoulos lined up for every day of the week, all at once Kendra's hate ran out. She faced the fact then that Damon, her love for him, and the knowledge that he cared absolutely nothing for her, were at the root of why she wanted to leave. She went hot all over at the thought that he might have gleaned some idea that she cared for him, and suddenly it became imperative that she depart without delay. On that instant, Kendra took out her suitcase and began to pack.

For courtesy's sake she had to wait until the morning before she told anyone she was leaving. But her plan to tell Eugene, her host, that she was going home that day backfired when, at breakfast, Costas told her that his father had left very early to pay a visit to the nursing home.

'Faye's still all right?' she asked quickly, her frustration at having missed Eugene taking a rear seat in the sudden panic that Faye might still be in trouble.

'Quite all right,' Costas assured her cheerfully. 'I only spoke with my father for a few minutes before he rushed off, but already this morning they have been on the telephone to each other.' He paused to smile a gentle smile as though to say that, in love himself, he fully understood how that tremendous emotion could affect one. 'I think my father is planning to take her somewhere for a long holiday until the baby is born,' he added.

'Talking of holidays,' Kendra grabbed at his unwitting cue, 'mine is over.'

Costas stared at her with a puzzled expression. 'I'm not sure I understand what you are saying?'

There was only one way to say it, Kendra realised, and did just that. 'I'm going home today,' she told him.

'You're...' Staggered by her sudden announcement, Costas stared at her. 'Does my father know?' he asked in complete surprise.

'That's why I particularly wanted to see him this morning. However...' An hour and a half later, Kendra was seated in Athens airport and was thinking of how relatively simple it had been once she had said those words, 'I'm going home today'.

Costas had protested at first but, hoping that he knew nothing of how Damon had seen to it that she had no job to go home to, she had explained that she was a working girl and that she had already taken one extra day's holiday. To her relief Costas had seemed to think that she had taken the extra day on account of Faye's being hospitalised, and he was all co-operation after that.

'I'll drive you to the airport,' he had told her, and, assuming that she had her passage home booked, had asked, 'What time is your flight?'

Because she did not want any fuss, nor did she want him having more time off work on her account than necessary, she had avoided giving him an exact time, but had implied that it would not be a bad idea if they left for the airport now.

There had been a small hitch at the airport when Costas had wanted to wait with her until it was time for her to go through into the departure lounge. But, since she had not yet so much as made enquiries about a plane home, she did not want to invite complication at this stage.

'I'm sure you must have plenty to do at your office,' she smiled, and, handing him a hastily scribbled note, she asked him to give it to either Faye or his father, and wished Costas all the very best of luck with his love Obelia. At which Costas gave her an affectionate hug, and, kissing her on both cheeks, he left, whereupon Kendra went to make enquiries about a flight.

Everyone, it seemed, was anxious to get to England that day. But she was lucky in that, even though it involved quite a delay, she managed to book out on a flight that was due to take off around two that afternoon.

With hours of waiting stretching before her, Kendra went and sat down and tried desperately to keep thoughts of Damon out of her head. She tried to concentrate on how she would by far have preferred to have said her thanks to Eugene in person. She wasn't very happy at all to have repaid his hospitality with the sketchy note which she had given to Costas. She was not very happy at all about... Her thoughts broke off, for that was the truth, she was not very happy at all.

She swallowed hard on a knot of emotion in her throat. Oh, Damon, Damon, Damon, she thought, and could have wept that when she wanted above all else to stay forever where he was, she was having to run away.

Aghast when weak, shaming tears pricked her eyes, Kendra became horrified lest anyone among the people milling about should see them. Hurriedly, she made a study of her feet and stayed studying them until she had gained control from that quite dreadful moment.

Before she could start to raise her eyes from the floor, though, another pair of shoes had come to join hers almost toe to toe. They were well-made shoes, and not at all like the trainers and casual footwear which most people around seemed to have adopted. And suddenly, without knowing why, Kendra began to feel apprehensive.

Her eyes took in the expensive cloth of the trouser-legs above the shoes and, as a premonition took her, her heart, with no sane reason, started to hurry its beat. Swiftly then, needing to know and thereby be back to normal again, Kendra jerked her head the rest of the way up. Then her mind became a kaleidoscope of memories, among them how she and this man had stood nearly naked with each other, and her face went scarlet.

She opened her mouth and, even while she was too stunned to find any reason why Damon should be there, she was glad of that pride which arrived to pop impudent words on her tongue. 'Come to speed me on my way?' she drawled. She saw his expression tighten at her manner, but she had to scotch any idea he might have that she in any way cared for him. He must never know what it was doing to her to see him there so unexpectedly.

'Far from coming to speed you on your way,' Damon clipped harshly, 'I have come to stop you from leaving.'

'Huh!' Kendra began, stubbornness joining pride as she prepared to tell him that he'd had a wasted journey. Suddenly though, her brain started to wake up from the stunned shock it had been in. Giving herself a mental shake, she realised that by no stretch of the imagination would Damon come chasing after her on his own behalf. 'Faye...' she whispered. 'Is Faye...'

'Your cousin...' Panic hit Kendra when he broke off as if choosing the right words. 'Faye,' he said after a second or two, 'wants to see you.'

'She's...' The words 'all right' didn't get said. For, as if he wanted to waste no further time in getting her to the nursing home, Damon hefted up her suitcase. Then, with her suitcase in one hand, he took hold of Kendra's right arm with the other. And, all before she had time or wind to protest, he had marched her out to his car.

Feeling certain that things must have started to go badly wrong for Faye and the baby again—though why Faye was asking to see her Kendra could not fathom—they were driving well away from the airport before she got her breath back.

Putting from her the memory of how Damon, as surly as he was now, had collected her from the airport once before, Kendra hoped with all her heart that all was well with Faye and the baby.

Damon was steering his car into a wide tree-lined street which was by now familiar to Kendra, as she grew more and more anxious beside him. He was actually pulling up outside Eugene's villa, though, before she uttered a word.

'Faye's home?' she gasped in some surprise, only to realise that she could have saved her breath. Damon, it seemed, was not in a question-answering mood that day.

At least, that was the way it seemed when, ignoring her question and with a hand on her arm once more, he escorted her into the villa. Her question was still unanswered as he issued some instruction to the hovering Medea, and took Kendra not to the private suite of Faye and Eugene but to the general sitting-room.

Then it was that he let go his hold on her arm. Then it was that, in tones not very friendly, he deigned to answer her question.

'So far as I know,' he said shortly, 'Faye Themelis is still in the nursing home where she was the last time you saw her.'

'But . . .' Kendra gasped, searching for comprehension '. . . if Faye wants to see me—why have you brought me here?' His answer was to shake her rigid.

'Your cousin, as far as I'm aware, had made no particular request to see you today,' he coolly informed her, and, as Kendra stared at him with ever-widening green eyes, 'I brought you here,' he went on to answer her next question, 'because in the light of past experience, it seemed to me safer to bring you to this house than to take you to mine.' And while Kendra stared at him, he told her sternly, 'I brought you here because one look at your stubborn expression at the airport was all I needed to know that, unless I took action of some sort, you would never let me say a word of what is burning in me to be said.'

Suddenly Kendra's mouth went dry. Usually she was a quick thinker, but Damon seemed to have changed all that. 'What...?' she asked, and found, the word coming out chokily, that she could not even get her question framed.

It was then that she began to see a gentler side of Damon. 'Come,' he said quietly, the short tone gone from his voice as he took hold of her arm and led her to a settee. Urging her to be seated, he sat down beside her. Then he said softly, 'Do not be alarmed, my dear.'

But Kendra *was* alarmed. Suddenly her ability to think quickly was going into erratic overdrive. Why was Damon calling her 'my dear'? Had he seen that she loved him? He must have done! What was more, if she was reading this correctly, had he hauled her back from the airport to—what—proposition her? Did he have it in mind that she should be his—mistress? It couldn't be that—could it?

CHAPTER NINE

'ALARMED?' Kendra drawled, inwardly panicking wildly, but pride insisting that she appear outwardly calm. 'Why, for heaven's sake, should I be alarmed? Just because you've seen fit to lie...'

'A lie, a small lie, was necessary,' Damon cut across her words just as Kendra was building up a fine head of sarcastic steam.

'Well, that shouldn't bother you,' she retorted.

'You're implying I've lied on other occasions?' he asked puzzled.

'You...' she began to challenge, but as she thought hard, save for that green-eyed jealous doubt that Rhodeia Stassinopoulos was more his friend than his sister's, she had no proof of any other lie he had told her. '*Small* lie!' she erupted, having to resort to challenging him over the one lie she did have proof of. 'How dared you let me believe that Faye was again in danger of losing her baby? How d...'

'Forgive me,' Damon cut her off. 'I'd no idea your imagination would travel to such areas. When I told you that your cousin wished to see you, I meant only to...'

'Well, Faye doesn't want to see me!' Kendra cut him off shortly, 'So, since I should much prefer to be checking in prior to catching my flight back to England rather than sitting here with you, I should be very much obliged if you would take me straight back to the airport.' With that, she would have shot to her feet and marched from the settee. Would have, had not Damon read her intention and, moving more quickly than she, captured her wrist in a firm hold.

'Did you not hear me say that I brought you here because there are—things—which I must say to you?' he asked, having effectively prevented her from going anywhere.

If her memory served her correctly, he had said that he had something in him that was burning to be said. But Kendra was overwhelmingly aware of her vulnerability where he was concerned, and even while part of her admitted to a curiosity, her fear that he might have seen her love, or that she might unthinkingly give herself away, caused her to still want to be making for the airport with all speed.

'What in creation makes you think that I'd be remotely interested in anything you have to say?' she exclaimed aloofly, and made an attempt to jerk her wrist free from his hold.

She saw a dull flush of colour creep up beneath his skin, but she was certain it was not caused by any emotion he experienced at hearing that she didn't give a damn about anything he had to say. He held on firmly to her, however, while he told her manfully, 'After the way I've behaved with you, I suppose I should be surprised if you were at all interested.'

'If you're referring to the way you very nearly seduced me on Saturday night...' Abruptly, Kendra broke off. She hadn't meant to say that, she hadn't! She looked from him, realising that by the clever way he had agreed that she should not be interested in what he said he had defeated her in one argument, only to goad her into another subject for argument. A subject which she would have said she'd die rather than bring up.

'I was not referring to Saturday night alone,' Damon said, placing a forefinger on her cheek to turn her face round so that he could look into her eyes. Quickly Kendra lowered her lashes, because, notwithstanding his scorching hold on her wrist, just the touch of one finger on her cheek was sending her all topsy-turvy. 'Although, up until then, I confess, I was certain that you had lain with at least one lover.'

'If you mean Nigel Robinson,' Kendra chipped in, though she had been fully resolved not to utter another word, 'then I can only tell you that you should have listened when I told you ages ago he was a friend.'

'You did tell me that,' he again agreed. Though this time he qualified, 'Although you didn't answer me when I specifically asked you if he were your lover. From your non-answer, I was sure you were telling me that he was.'

Kendra shrugged her shoulders as if to say, what difference does it make? and would have turned her head from him again. The thought, though, that he might a second time weaken her by touching her cheek made her stay facing him. 'So now you know,' she said unconcernedly, ready to risk trying to get to her feet again. If Damon would not take her back to the airport, she would soon see about taking a taxi.

But Damon was holding determinedly on to her and, when she had no intention of entering further argument, she just found it impossible to let his next remark pass. 'Yes, I now know,' he murmured. 'I now know that not only have you no knowledge of a man's bed, but you are as innocent of all I have thought and have accused you of.'

'It took you until Saturday night to see that, did it?' she retorted, finding herself unable to keep quiet, and not thanking him for his sudden insight. 'It took you until then—until you'd nearly got me into your bed—to...' Again Kendra came to an abrupt halt. She looked into his watching dark eyes and as, side-tracked, she recalled being near-naked in his arms that night, warm colour flooded her face.

'Kendra,' Damon said softly, and raised one hand to gently touch the curve of her hot cheek.

But Kendra did not want his touch, his weakening touch. Neither, as she jerked her head away, did she want him talking of... Her thoughts broke off mid-stream, for suddenly, as what he had said played back in her head, she was realising what all this was about. Suddenly, as it began to penetrate that he had said he believed her innocent of all he had thought and accused her of, she realised why Damon had come chasing to the airport after her. He had not come chasing after her with a view to propositioning her at all—she must have been crazy, in her panic that he must not see her love, to have ever thought so. As relief hit her that he could not have seen the love she had for him, her vision widened and she was able to see that the only reason Damon had come to stop her going to England was that he was a man of honour. A man of honour who would not offend against a relative's house no matter how distant that relationship happened to be. She had no need to look beyond the way he had ceased making love to her when he had discovered she was a virgin to know that! Quite clearly, Damon believed he would offend Eugene and his house if he allowed her to return to England before he had given her his apology in person for past thoughts and words.

'It's taken you until now to see that I'm none of the things you thought me, has it?' she flared, not sure why she was feeling piqued, but certainly not experiencing any loving feeling of wanting to make his apology easy for him. But already Damon was shaking his head.

'There were clear signs before, which I deliberately chose to ignore,' he admitted, and further confessed, somewhat to her surprise, 'Your genuine embarrassment, not to mention your indignation, when on your first Sunday in my country I would have loaned you the currency you did not have, was without question. Yet,' he revealed, 'I, in my stubbornness to believe only what I wanted to believe about you, was soon discounting that there had been anything genuine in your reaction.'

'Because you'd already pre-decided that I was after any man who was in the least wealthy,' Kendra snapped, not thanking him for his confession. 'You were too high and mighty,' she warmed to her theme, 'to give a moment's thought to the possibility that you might be wrong about me!' As her fury started to soar, she would have surged on, but suddenly Damon was chipping in, and what he said was effective in totally neutralising her anger.

'I wouldn't have thought it possible, but you're even more beautiful when you're angry,' he told her, and while Kendra stared, silent, if open-mouthed, he took advantage of the way he had weakened her to astonish her by saying, 'A mere apology is not sufficient. Nothing will do, since so much depends upon it, but that I risk your scorn and begin by telling you how, from the moment of our first meeting, I set my heart against you.'

She was not sure that her jaw did not drop further, but, as her eyes widened and she thought of the moment of their first meeting, all she could find to say was a weak, 'But our first meeting was at Faye's wedding and you didn't know the first thing about me then!' Her voice grew stronger, however, when as realisation dawned on her she questioned coolly, 'Oh, I see it! Charming! You took one look, decided that I was—I was—on the make, and...'

'I've said a mere apology is not enough,' Damon cut in, frowning and clearly not liking the coolness of her tone. 'Your cousin is blonde and beautiful and, forgive me, Kendra, but without question she was marrying Eugene for his wealth. He...'

'Faye loves Eugene, very much,' Kendra spurted in, cutting him off to defend her cousin. 'She told me so only yesterday, although anyone could have seen yesterday how heart and soul in love with him she is!' she added, working herself up to be angry with Damon again.

'If you say so, I believe you,' he said mildly, his slightly teasing tone at her vehemence causing her to feel she had overdone it with her outburst.

'Well...' she said lamely.

'Well, indeed,' he said gently and, determined, it seemed, to explain fully that which a 'mere apology' would not cover, he went back to what he was saying before her outburst. 'I had met Faye the evening prior to her marriage,' he resumed. 'Then, the very next day, while knowing that were Eugene without money none of us would be there—a blonder and even more beautiful woman than his fiancée enters the room.' Kendra was quiet, her eyes serious on his when he added, 'There was nothing I could do to prevent my totally besotted relative from getting tied up with a woman who wanted him only for his money, but, my dear,' he said, that 'my dear' causing Kendra to dig her nails into her palms as she fought to keep her expression unaltered, 'there was a great deal I could do to see to it that I—didn't go along the same route.'

Staggered, Kendra had no chance of keeping her face expressionless. But even as her jaw fell open, a feeling came over her that Damon was playing some game here which would leave her coming off a second best, and she drew on every scrap of indignation to drawl haughtily, not to say sarcastically, 'You do rather flatter yourself, Damon, *my dear*. For the life of me, I've no recollection whatsoever of giving you any sign that I had any interest in you, or your bank balance, at that wedding.'

She saw a muscle move in his temple as that hit home, but, even loving him as she did, Kendra could not regret what she had said—she had to keep him from knowing how she had started to fall in love with him at that first meeting.

'I deserved that,' he said, after a moment or two of silence. 'But,' he went on, 'were you not so innocent in these matters, you'd have appreciated that the polite but aloof way you behaved to me that day could well have been seen as your way of getting me to do something to change your attitude.'

'Good heavens!' she exclaimed faintly. 'You mean—I could have been seen as—encouraging you!'

'I didn't make that mistake,' he quickly set her mind at rest. 'Though many were the mistakes I made afterwards.'

'You—surprise me,' Kendra told him, doing her best to sound sarcastic, as if she could never imagine him making a single mistake, much less confess to one.

He did surprise her, though, in that he bore her sarcasm very well, and even went on to illustrate, 'The first mistake I made was to decide to return home the very next day. The next mistake to was decide to cut you out of my thoughts—and out of my life.'

In opposition to a heart that had suddenly decided to go crazy, Kendra opted to ignore the second part of what he had said. For surely such a statement about cutting her out of his thoughts and out of his life could only be part and parcel of Damon's stringing her along for some obscure reason which could only hold grief for her at the end of it.

'You weren't intending to return home the day after Faye's wedding?' she enquired, half of her wondering why in creation she was sitting there if she knew that there was going to be nothing but grief at the end of this—for the want of a better word—chat. While the other half of her knew that, self-indulgent though it might be, she did not care what happened, she just had to have a few minutes longer with Damon—the future was going to be bleak anyway.

'I had a few days more on my work schedule before I returned to Athens,' Damon replied, 'and would have stayed to complete that schedule—had not Costas annoyed me by trying to date you.'

'Costas!' she exclaimed, wondering what he had to do with anything—until she remembered. Again she made an angry movement to get her wrist free, and gave such a violent jerk that only by hurting her could Damon have continued to hold on to her. 'Pardon me for forgetting,' she said stiffly, but unable to contain her fury. 'My God!' she exploded. 'You couldn't wait to warn me off the night you met me at the airport, either, could you? I hadn't been in your country an hour when you were telling me to leave him alone!'

'There are so many things I should ask your forgiveness for,' Damon again cooled her fire by, with some charm, agreeing that she had a right to be angry. 'But the truth of the matter is that, while I tried to convince myself that it was for Costas's sake that I must do what I could to sever any romantic attachment between the two of you, it was, as I now willingly accept, for my sake that I did what I did.'

'For—your sake?' Kendra queried warily, and she was so concerned, as nerves got to her, with wondering what he was up to that Damon had taken a hold of her hand without her doing anything to stop him.

'Although I wasn't admitting it at the time,' he confessed, 'I was—jealous.'

Instinctively, Kendra went to pull her hand out of his hold, but he had it in a firm grip, and she was forced to let it lie. But as she stared into his sincere dark eyes her throat went dry, and the word, 'Jealous?' left her on something of a cracked note.

'I'm afraid so,' he told her without hesitation. And, when she still appeared too dumbstruck to say anything else, he went on to admit freely, 'Jealousy, when I heard Costas trying to arrange to see you again at his father's wedding, was the sole reason for my making the immediate decision that we would fly back to Greece the following day.'

'I c-can't believe it!' Kendra told him chokily, while her heart thundered and, even if she was convinced that grief would be hers at the end of this interview, nothing could have made her leave for the airport until she had heard more.

'Neither could I,' Damon told her quietly, and had somehow acquired a hold on her other hand too, as he went on, 'I was still refusing to believe I had experienced any such emotion when, six months later, Eugene announced that you were coming to stay, and I experienced that self-same feeling again when Costas at once volunteered to meet you at the airport.'

'You were again—jealous?' she questioned, some unnumbed part of her putting the words into her mouth.

'It didn't take me long to find him some work to do well away from Athens,' Damon smiled.

His smile did funny things to her insides and made it more difficult than ever for Kendra to try and sort out where this apology was heading. 'Oh,' she murmured, as she played for time. 'I—er—I'd never have known when you—er—took Costas's place and met me, that you'd felt—er—anything remotely like jealousy where I was concerned.'

'You were not intended to, sweet Kendra,' Damon said softly, the warmth in the dark eyes that stared into hers enough to melt her bones without the 'sweet Kendra'. Try as she might, however, she could not find one single word of reply, and her heartbeats were erratic again when he went on, 'I had to deny to myself how attracted I'd been to you at Eugene's wedding. Just as I...'

'You were attracted to me at...!' Kendra's new-found voice faded as shock took her. But it grew strong again as she challenged, 'My memory of you was that you were anything *but* attracted to me!'

'Which was the impression I preferred you to have,' he said quietly.

Kendra thought for a while, but, finding the answers she sought difficult to unearth, she just had to ask, 'Why?'

'Have you not seen Eugene, and how he lives only for Faye?'

'Y-yes,' Kendra admitted.

'Then could you blame me, when I saw how it was with him on his wedding day, that I should decide that no woman was going to have me that way about her?' Staring at him, Kendra could hardly believe Damon was intimating that he feared she might have the same power over him that Faye had over Eugene. Searching for enlightenment as to what Damon *did* mean, however, she was shaken yet again when he quietly disclosed, 'I decided when Costas and I left England the next morning that I was going to cut you out of my mind, my thoughts. I was doing fairly well, too,' he smiled, 'and then Faye started to give Eugene a hard time. I knew I was in trouble when life seemed suddenly brighter for me when he declared that you had agreed to come and cheer your cousin up.'

'Is—er—that so?' Kendra murmured, quite idiotically she thought; though with her heart going like a trip hammer, and with Damon being so gentle and charming to her, and even smiling encouragingly at her sometimes, she was not surprised that she should utter something inane.

'I assure you it is,' he said softly. 'Forgive me, my dear,' he went on, ignorant of the way his 'my dear' had made her heart race, 'that I found it necessary to convince myself you were cast in the same money-orientated mould as your cousin.'

The time had come, Kendra knew, when she must assert herself and tell him that she did not care a light what he had convinced himself of. But, when she opened her mouth to do just that, the actual words to leave her were a husky-sounding, 'Why—did you find it necessary to do anything of the sort?'

Feeling betrayed by her own tongue, Kendra looked from him to the hold his hands had on hers. Her hands were still in his when she saw his grip tighten and his knuckles go white—just as if he was striving for some inner control. Her eyes flew to his, though, when he began, 'Darling Kendra. Sweet, innocent love, have you not reasoned yet how it is with me?'

She shook her head. Her throat went dry as she tried to read what lay in that look he gave her—what lay in the words he had said. 'Am I-I being p-particularly dim?' she asked huskily.

Damon smiled, 'How could anyone know you and not love you,' he said, taking her breath away.

'Y-you love—*me*?' she croaked with what wind she had left to speak.

'Love, my dearest Kendra, is understating what I feel for you,' he confessed, and there was a hoarse kind of note in his voice when he went on, 'I adore you, little one. I love you, am in love with you, and will know no rest until you are mine.'

'Oh!' Kendra gasped, joy, unbelievable joy starting to break in her. Even if she did not fully comprehend what he was meaning, it was enough, more than enough, to know just then that—dared she believe it?—Damon loved her!

One look at his strained expression, though, was sufficient to tell her that he felt something very strongly for her. For he seemed to be waiting in some torment for what she would reply. Confirmation of his mental anguish came when it appeared that he could wait no longer when she found nothing more to say after her exclaimed 'Oh!'

'Is it all right with you that I love you, Kendra?' he pressed urgently.

'Oh, yes,' she whispered, feeling suddenly shy.

She expected he might smile, or at least give some indication that her answer had pleased him. But he did not smile, but looked quite severe.

'And...' he paused, and seemed to need to draw a long breath before he completed '...my proposal meets with—your favour?'

His proposal! Staring at him, with her green eyes overlarge in her face, Kendra could hardly believe her hearing. Some of her uprush of joy began to evaporate, though, when, trying to think just when he had proposed marriage, she realised that he had not done so.

She was never more glad then that she had not burst out into rapturous smiles. For, having thought over the events of Saturday night enough times to have instant recall, she realised that her earlier thoughts that he had brought her back from the airport to proposition her had been exactly on target.

'You want me to be your mistress?' she asked, for pride's sake trying hard not to let him see how suddenly let down she was feeling.

She was not left feeling let down for long, though. Because, with his expression little short of outraged at the very idea, Damon was exclaiming, '*Theos! No!* That's not what I want at all!'

'But . . .' she began to protest, not liking the feeling he gave her that she had said something particularly scandalous '. . . you asked me to be yours on S-Saturday night, and . . . and the only proposal I've heard since is when you just said that you won't know any rest until I'm yours. I . . .' She broke off, defeated.

But her heart was soon singing, and she was once more overjoyed, when Damon told her stiffly, 'You will also recall that I've told you how very much in love with you I am. I would not,' he said firmly, 'say that to any woman other than the woman I intend to marry.'

A trembling began somewhere inside her as the message started to get through that Damon *had* proposed marriage. 'Oh!' she said shakily, but was still having a hard time taking it in.

Some of his colour had gone when, 'Well?' he rapped, not at all lover-like, she thought. 'Will you?' he questioned shortly, and only then did she realise why he was sounding so unlover-like. Unbelievably, Damon was nervous!

'Yes, I will,' she said promptly.

'Will marry me?' he queried, unsmiling, as if he now needed to make sure that she fully understood what he was asking.

'I'll marry you whenever you say,' Kendra told him, and watched as the most wonderful smile started to break on him.

'Then, my darling,' he murmured as he started to pull her closer up to him, 'that can only mean that you love me.'

'Why do you say that?' she asked shyly.

'I know enough about you now, my dear one,' he breathed, 'to know that you would never marry a man for any reason other than love.'

Kendra had time only to answer, 'You're right, of course,' and then he was holding her close up against his heart.

For a little while after that, time ceased to have any meaning, and in between planting ardent kisses all over her face Damon would pull back just to look at her, when words of endearment in Greek and in English would leave him.

His heart seemed to be as full as Kendra's when, breaking one long and exquisite kiss to her parted lips, he murmured, 'Oh, my dear, dear love!'

'Am I dreaming?' Kendra asked him softly, and was kissed again.

Shaking his head at the love-filled look in her eyes when next he pulled back from her, he breathed, 'Why you love me is past my understanding,' a heavy emotional note there in his throaty voice.

'It's a mystery to me too,' she gently teased him, but had to confess, 'Though I've been very much aware of you from the very beginning.'

'How could you be otherwise?' he asked, keeping her tenderly enfolded in his arms. 'I don't think it's every day you go to happily enjoy a wedding only to meet someone as sour as I was to you that day.'

'You knew you were being sour?'

'My self-protective instincts were already warning me that you were going to cause me many lost hours of sleep.'

'You too? I mean,' Kendra smiled, 'I didn't know that you too...'

'Spent sleepless nights thinking of my love,' Damon finished for her, and went on to tell her, 'I've been thoroughly unsettled from the moment I met you off your plane and tried to deny to myself how very much beneath my skin you were.'

'Really?' Kendra asked happily, her heart full to overflowing.

'Of course,' he said, as if there was no disputing the fact. 'From then on you turned my life upside down.'

'Did I?' Kendra asked delightedly, and absolutely adored the way he laughed as though he too was absolutely delighted—with her. 'How?' she asked.

'Well,' he said, 'to begin with I'd brought you here in the early hours of Saturday morning but with no intention of seeing you again before you returned to England. Then, even as I got ready to decline Eugene's invitation to come to dinner that night, I caught you almost purring at the thought that I would do just that, and the next thing I knew...'

'You'd accepted,' Kendra finished for him.

'Exactly,' he said, and with a lift of one brow, 'More?' he teased.

'Yes, please,' she said, and felt she would never tire of hearing how it had been with him when, settling her more comfortably in his arms, he went on,

'So I came to dinner that night and, although your manners were above reproach, I was inwardly irritated that plainly you didn't care whether I was there or not. Which, of course, was why I decided that not once was

I going to call on Eugene's house again until you had returned whence you came.'

'But you called—the very next day!' Kendra exclaimed. 'After we'd had lunch that Sunday, you called and...'

'Of course I did,' he smiled. 'I should have admitted defeat then, my darling,' he said tenderly. 'Forgive me, dear love, but having spent half the night in reasserting to myself that you were set in the same avaricious mould as your cousin, I still had to come that afternoon.'

'You took me to the Acropolis,' she smiled, 'when Costas couldn't take me because of the work...' Her voice faded, something in Damon's expression causing her to break off. 'You... devil,' she laughed. 'It wasn't that vital that Costas went into the office that Sunday afternoon, was it?'

'See what jealousy will do to a man?' Damon replied, and kissed her surprise-parted lips simply because he could not stop himself. 'I wasn't having him taking you to the Acropolis,' he told her.

'Oh, Damon!' Kendra sighed, and gently she kissed him, was kissed in return, and was again snuggled up in his arms when he lovingly revealed,

'You enchanted me more and more at the Acropolis when your eyes shone with your pleasure at all you were seeing. You told me you thought it was unforgettable,' he reminded her, 'and I knew, then, that so were you. It was then,' he confessed, 'that I started to see the real you as opposed to the you which my self-protective instincts were insisting I saw.'

Kendra remembered how she had felt in harmony with him, and told him so. 'Although it didn't last, did it?' she added quietly, as she remembered how in stony silence they had returned to the villa.

'How could it last, sweet love?' Damon asked. 'Had you not given me a very clear impression that your friend Nigel Robinson was your lover?'

'You were jealous of Nigel too!'

'As jealous as hell,' Damon admitted softly. 'Though when you made the effort to thank me for the afternoon, something in me just could not let you go until we'd made friends.'

'You told me the pleasure was all yours,' she recalled happily; if she was dreaming never wanting to wake up. Never had she thought to be able to talk so freely with Damon. Never had she ever thought that he would tell her that he loved her. And never, ever, had she thought he would ask her to marry him.

'And pleasure it was, darling Kendra,' he said. 'Which is why I deliberately stayed away from Eugene's house for the next few days.'

'Because...'

'Because I was liking you too well,' Damon supplied. 'Because I was enjoying your company too well. And because I knew I was getting in too deeply when I realised that I was ready to be jealous of any man who had ever looked at you. When I began to fear for your life, I knew that I was in love with you.'

'Fear for my life!'

'I was as mad as fury when one night around midnight Eugene rang and said that Costas had taken you to Delphi, but that you weren't back yet.'

'You were mad because we were late back and caused Eugene so much anxiety?' Kendra queried.

'I was mad because you were *supposed* to go to Delphi *with me*!'

'But you never...'

'I know I never made any arrangement to take you, but that didn't stop me from being furious that you had gone there with Costas.' Suddenly Damon grinned, and Kendra's heart danced merry cartwheels. 'See how entirely unreasonable being in love can make you?'

'You knew then that you were in love with me, you said,' Kendra reminded him, and received a gentle kiss on her brow before he explained how Eugene had phoned him that night on the off-chance that she and Costas had called in on him on their way back from Delphi.

'I put the phone down telling myself that I didn't give a damn whether you and Costas never got home. But, an hour later, there I am getting my car out and taking a drive over here.'

'Eugene was still up.'

Damon nodded. 'Most of the downstairs lights seemed to be on, so I came in and waited with Eugene, telling him the whole while that of course you and Costas would be all right. While, at the same time,' he went on, 'I was growing more and more concerned. When I found myself thinking in terms of doing Costas some serious injury if he had so much as harmed one hair on your head, I could no longer hide from the fact that you had come to be my world.'

'Oh, darling!' Kendra cried, and their lips met in a gently loving and giving kiss. 'But,' she said some minutes later, 'as I remember it, you were more furious than loving when you saw me.'

'How else should I be?' he asked softly. 'Costas had taken you to the one place above all others that I wanted to take you, and there are you—after giving me a couple of hours of pure hell as I waited—coming in and telling Costas that you thought Delphi was absolutely out of this world!'

'I'm sorry,' Kendra said, and was truly contrite, as she reminded him, 'You accused me of leading Costas astray.'

'I didn't accuse you without getting paid, did I?' Damon smiled. 'You hit me.'

'And you kissed me.'

'And, as you returned my kiss, I was stunned by a never before known feeling of wanting to protect someone for the rest of my life.'

'Oh, Damon,' she whispered, and some minutes passed before she asked, 'You weren't ready then to tell me how you felt?'

He shook his head. 'I never knew that such an emotion could so turn a man's world on its head. I was in love with you, I knew that for a fact, but my self-protective instinct was still insisting that I should not go the same besotted way as my friend and relative, Eugene. He was up to the top of his head in love with his English bride, but from what I observed he was receiving little happiness from being in love. Why should I fare any differently?' he asked, and immediately apologised, 'Forgive me that I had to take a hard-headed view of my situation.'

'What did your hard-headed view bring you?'

'No more joy than my soft-headed one,' he divulged. 'The hard-headed, not to say jealous part of me had soon seen that the only reason you had pulled out of my arms and raced away was because you'd heard the study door open and didn't want Costas to find you in my arms.'

'Good heavens!' Kendra could not help exclaiming, such a thing never having occurred to her.

Damon's forefinger traced the gentle curving surprise on her mouth as he confessed, 'I had to find a way to let you know that I was still very much my own man.'

'Ah,' said Kendra, because, suddenly, something had clicked. 'Is that why you introduced me to Rhodeia Stassinopoulos?'

'You're quick,' Damon grinned, as he owned, 'There was no need for me to call on Eugene that night, but since I was taking Astrea's friend out to dine...'

'You thought you'd call in to show me that I wasn't the only pebble on the beach.'

'Something like that,' Damon agreed. 'Although all I got for my pains was another serving of jealousy. To my mind, you were standing much too close to Costas as we left.'

'Had you but known it, Damon, my dear Damon,' Kendra said softly, 'I was so consumed by jealousy when you introduced me to Rhodeia that I knew then why from the very first you had been able to affect my emotions.'

'You realised then that you were in love with me?' he asked incredulously. Kendra beamed a smile at him and nodded.

A breathless few minutes later, they broke their kiss and Damon went on to tell her how he had been able to settle to nothing after the time he'd held her responsive in his arms. He told of how, when Costas had come in to work one morning and had mentioned that he had dropped her off in Omonia Square, nothing would do but that he had to come looking for her.

'You weren't at that bank by accident when I came out!' Kendra gasped, and she knew more delight when Damon admitted that there had been nothing accidental about that meeting.

'My heart was thumping from just seeing you. Though when I gave in to the need to spend a few more minutes with you and asked you to have coffee with me, you, heartless creature, gave me your English cold-shoulder treatment. Can you wonder that I came nearer and nearer to knowing that I was going to have to do something fairly drastic about you?'

'What did you decide?'

'At that precise time my brain was tied up in so many differing and contradicting knots about you that no satisfactory plan would come. Then I received the heart-lifting news that you had agreed to stay until Faye's baby is born. Having casually pressed Eugene for a few relevant facts, such as who your employers were, I made a phone call to England.'

'The phone call that made me so furious?'

'That's the one,' he grinned. 'I didn't want you to have any excuse to return to England before I was ready.'

'You were still plotting something dark and devious for me?' she asked.

'In all honesty, my dearest love,' he told her, 'I can only answer that with a yes. Though I didn't know at the time,' he quickly added, 'that you were not worldly and knowledgeable about men.'

'You planned . . .' Kendra began, but she had to shake her head. 'I'm afraid I'm not much good at devious plans.'

'That doesn't surprise me,' he told her warmly, but went on to reveal, 'With you so much in my heart and my mind, I planned that the quickest way to get you out of both would be to take you to my bed.'

'You—er—um—very nearly succeeded on Saturday,' she put in haltingly. But only to realise that she had got something wrong when Damon started to shake his head.

'There was nothing pre-planned about Saturday night,' he told her gently. 'My plan to satiate my lust by making you mine and thereby getting you out of my head never left the ground.'

'It didn't?' she queried, feeling a trifle confused.

'In the first instance, it's not lust I feel for you, but love,' he set about clearing her confusion. 'In the second instance, when on Friday I accepted Eugene's invitation to dine with the express purpose of getting you on your own, no sooner were we alone than my words were coming out all wrong. After the casual, uncaring sound of the way I asked you out, I wasn't at all surprised that you as good as told me what I could do with my invitation.'

'I rang you the next morning, though,' Kendra reminded him, and he grinned again.

'You'll never know how thrilled I was to pick up the phone and to hear your voice. It took all my efforts not to show how pleased I was when you told me how you'd condescend to let me take you out for the day after all.'

Remembering that day and how that day had ended, Kendra just had to query, 'But you didn't intend... I mean, you said that there was nothing pre-planned in the way—um...'

'In the way I so nearly took you to my bed?' Damon butted in to spare her blushes. 'There wasn't, not then,' he confirmed, and went on to explain, 'The idea might still have been in my mind when I called for you on Saturday morning. Doubly so, perhaps, when such an overpowering jealousy bombarded me to see you holding hands with Costas in the garden.'

'You looked—er—fairly murderous,' Kendra told him, 'but I thought it was on account of your not wanting me to have anything to do with Costas.'

'I *didn't* want you to have anything to do with him,' Damon smiled. 'Though for my sake, not his, as I'd led you to believe. Anyhow,' he resumed, 'I was so enraged to see the two of you hand-holding that it was either come over and physically wrench your hands apart, or carry on walking.'

'You chose to carry on walking, and went on into the house,' Kendra documented, and he nodded, and told her,

'Eugene hailed me from the study as I went in. But when he told me his plans, and said that he intended to be away overnight, my plans in connection with taking you to my bed went far from my mind. All I knew then was that no way was I going to return you to Eugene's home where you would spend the night alone under the same roof as his hand-holding son.'

'Oh, Damon,' sighed Kendra, and could do no other than explain, 'Costas was only holding my hand out of some sort of need for comfort, as he told me how, the previous evening, he'd fallen in love at first sight—with someone else.' And, while Damon looked at her in some surprise, 'You'd no need to feel jealous of him at all,' she told him. Then, gently, she kissed him.

Gently, he returned her kiss. 'How nearly I took you in my arms that afternoon,' he murmured, as they looked into each other's eyes.

'At Epidaurus?' she questioned.

'It showed?' he queried with a smile.

'I thought I'd imagined it,' she smiled back at him.

'There was nothing imaginary about my emotions for you that day,' Damon told her, and confessed, 'It was a fact, my love, my life, that I fell more and more in love with you with every hour that passed. When later I discovered the true innocence of you, I was totally and utterly devastated. All I knew for certain in those first few minutes was that you would be far safer alone under the same roof as Costas—where there were live-in staff—than in my home with me.'

'You didn't—er—trust yourself?'

'That's an understatement!' he exclaimed with some feeling. 'Not only could I not trust myself with you, but I spent the whole of yesterday in hell, realising that I could no longer trust my judgement.'

'Poor love,' Kendra said softly, and as Damon brought her hand to his lips and kissed it, she asked, 'Is that why you didn't answer your phone yesterday?'

'You tried to ring me?'

'Costas did. He tried several times to contact you,' she explained.

'I wasn't home yesterday,' Damon told her. 'After I'd brought you back here on Saturday night, I took myself off to a place I have in the mountains, obsessed by you, for my sins, as I had never intended to be.'

Lovingly he pulled her closer to his heart and, content just to be with each other, they stayed like that for some while. Kendra felt that she never wanted his arms from about her as, talking quietly, she enquired, 'So you didn't know until this morning about Faye being taken to a nursing home?'

'My thoughts were on you and how I didn't want any woman to have the hold that you had, as I drove to Athens this morning,' Damon owned. 'I was still being consumed by thoughts of you when Costas came to my office to tell me of the family trauma of the weekend. Only when he referred to how he had just left you at the airport, however, did I instantly know that, whatever happened, I could not let you go out of my life. For you, my beautiful one, are my sun, my moon and my stars, and without you, for me, there is no life.' Kendra swallowed hard on a knot of emotion, and Damon ended, 'Costas was still speaking as I charged for the door. "Where are you going?" he called after me. "To marry Kendra, if she'll have me," I told him.'

'Oh—my dear!' she cried, her voice husky with the emotion she was feeling.

There was deep emotion in Damon's voice too when, taking his arms from around her, he sat facing her and gripped her hands tightly. 'Because of how I have been with you, I've bared my soul to you, dear love,' he breathed. 'But now, I can endure to wait no longer to hear the words which I feared you might never say, but which I am longing to hear.'

'I don't... I'm not sure...' Kendra began huskily, uncertainly.

'I love you,' Damon told her, and gave her a very large hint that although she had conveyed that she loved him, as yet she had not said so in as many words.

'Oh, my dear, dear Damon,' she whispered, 'I—l-love you, with all my heart.'

It had come out shakily, and shyly, for it was the first time she had ever said it. But it was what Damon wanted to hear. Gently he let go of her hands, and tenderly he gathered her once more into his arms—and held her. And, just as Kendra wanted, it seemed as though he would never let her go.

HARLEQUIN Romance

Coming Next Month

#3013 THE MARRYING GAME Lindsay Armstrong
Kirra's encounter with Matt Remington on a deserted beach is an episode she wants to forget. Then she learns Matt is the only one who can save her father's business—and only she can pay the price!

#3014 LOVING DECEIVER Katherine Arthur
Theresa would have preferred never to see scriptwriter Luke Thorndike again, let alone travel to New Orleans with him. Yet, although he'd hurt her badly five years ago, she just couldn't desert him now, when his life was in danger....

#3015 UNDER A SUMMER SUN Samantha Day
Anne is puzzled by Rob MacNeil's antagonism. After all, he's the interloper, taking the very piece of land that Anne had hoped to build on. She soon discovers that Rob is intruding on more than her land....

#3016 A PERFECT BEAST Kay Gregory
Rosemary's enjoyment in teaching is changed when sixteen-year-old Tamsin acts up. But the sparks that fly between Tamsin and Rosemary are nothing compared to those touched off by Rosemary's first meeting with Tamsin's father—the impossible Jonathan Riordan.

#3017 TROUBLEMAKER Madeleine Ker
Ginny was Ryan Savage's sweetheart when he was Grantly's teenage rebel, before he took off for big-city life. When he comes back five years later, Ginny, now engaged to an older, more responsible man, wonders what trouble he'll bring.

#3018 UNWILLING WOMAN Sue Peters
"Just elope," Jess had suggested jokingly to the young woman who didn't want to marry Max Beaumont—only to soon find herself trapped into becoming the unwilling Lady Blythe, wife of the arrogant but all-too-attractive Max....

Available in November wherever paperback books are sold, or through Harlequin Reader Service:

In the U.S.	In Canada
901 Fuhrmann Blvd.	P.O. Box 603
P.O. Box 1397	Fort Erie, Ontario
Buffalo, N.Y. 14240-1397	L2A 5X3

INDULGE A LITTLE SWEEPSTAKES

OFFICIAL RULES

SWEEPSTAKES RULES AND REGULATIONS. NO PURCHASE NECESSARY.

1. NO PURCHASE NECESSARY. To enter complete the official entry form and return with the invoice in the envelope provided. Or you may enter by printing your name, complete address and your daytime phone number on a 3 x 5 piece of paper. Include with your entry the hand printed words "Indulge A Little Sweepstakes." Mail your entry to: Indulge A Little Sweepstakes, P.O. Box 1397, Buffalo, NY 14269-1397. No mechanically reproduced entries accepted. Not responsible for late, lost, misdirected mail, or printing errors.

2. Three winners, one per month (Sept. 30, 1989, October 31, 1989 and November 30, 1989), will be selected in random drawings. All entries received prior to the drawing date will be eligible for that month's prize. This sweepstakes is under the supervision of MARDEN-KANE, INC. an independent judging organization whose decisions are final and binding. Winners will be notified by telephone and may be required to execute an affidavit of eligibility and release which must be returned within 14 days, or an alternate winner will be selected.

3. Prizes: 1st Grand Prize (1) a trip for two to Disneyworld in Orlando, Florida. Trip includes round trip air transportation, hotel accommodations for seven days and six nights, plus up to $700 expense money (ARV $3,500). 2nd Grand Prize (1) a seven-night Chandris Caribbean Cruise for two includes transportation from nearest major airport, accommodations, meals plus up to $1,000 in expense money (ARV $4,300). 3rd Grand Prize (1) a ten-day Hawaiian holiday for two includes round trip air transportation for two, hotel accommodations, sightseeing, plus up to $1,200 in spending money (ARV $7,700). All trips subject to availability and must be taken as outlined on the entry form.

4. Sweepstakes open to residents of the U.S. and Canada 18 years or older except employees and the families of Torstar Corp., its affiliates, subsidiaries and Marden-Kane, Inc. and all other agencies and persons connected with conducting this sweepstakes. All Federal, State and local laws and regulations apply. Void wherever prohibited or restricted by law. Taxes, if any are the sole responsibility of the prize winners. Canadian winners will be required to answer a skill testing question. Winners consent to the use of their name, photograph and/or likeness for publicity purposes without additional compensation.

5. For a list of prize winners, send a stamped, self-addressed envelope to Indulge A Little Sweepstakes Winners, P.O. Box 701, Sayreville, NJ 08871.

DL-SWPS

INDULGE A LITTLE SWEEPSTAKES

OFFICIAL RULES

SWEEPSTAKES RULES AND REGULATIONS. NO PURCHASE NECESSARY.

1. NO PURCHASE NECESSARY. To enter complete the official entry form and return with the invoice in the envelope provided. Or you may enter by printing your name, complete address and your daytime phone number on a 3 x 5 piece of paper. Include with your entry the hand printed words "Indulge A Little Sweepstakes." Mail your entry to: Indulge A Little Sweepstakes, P.O. Box 1397, Buffalo, NY 14269-1397. No mechanically reproduced entries accepted. Not responsible for late, lost, misdirected mail, or printing errors.

2. Three winners, one per month (Sept. 30, 1989, October 31, 1989 and November 30, 1989), will be selected in random drawings. All entries received prior to the drawing date will be eligible for that month's prize. This sweepstakes is under the supervision of MARDEN-KANE, INC. an independent judging organization whose decisions are final and binding. Winners will be notified by telephone and may be required to execute an affidavit of eligibility and release which must be returned within 14 days, or an alternate winner will be selected.

3. Prizes: 1st Grand Prize (1) a trip for two to Disneyworld in Orlando, Florida. Trip includes round trip air transportation, hotel accommodations for seven days and six nights, plus up to $700 expense money (ARV $3,500). 2nd Grand Prize (1) a seven-night Chandris Caribbean Cruise for two includes transportation from nearest major airport, accommodations, meals plus up to $1,000 in expense money (ARV $4,300). 3rd Grand Prize (1) a ten-day Hawaiian holiday for two includes round trip air transportation for two, hotel accommodations, sightseeing, plus up to $1,200 in spending money (ARV $7,700). All trips subject to availability and must be taken as outlined on the entry form.

4. Sweepstakes open to residents of the U.S. and Canada 18 years or older except employees and the families of Torstar Corp., its affiliates, subsidiaries and Marden-Kane, Inc. and all other agencies and persons connected with conducting this sweepstakes. All Federal, State and local laws and regulations apply. Void wherever prohibited or restricted by law. Taxes, if any are the sole responsibility of the prize winners. Canadian winners will be required to answer a skill testing question. Winners consent to the use of their name, photograph and/or likeness for publicity purposes without additional compensation

5. For a list of prize winners, send a stamped, self-addressed envelope to Indulge A Little Sweepstakes Winners, P.O. Box 701, Sayreville, NJ 08871.

© 1989 HARLEQUIN ENTERPRISES LTD

DL-SWPS

INDULGE A LITTLE—WIN A LOT!

Summer of '89 Subscribers-Only Sweepstakes

OFFICIAL ENTRY FORM

This entry must be received by: Sept. 30, 1989
This month's winner will be notified by: October 7, 1989
Trip must be taken between: Nov. 7, 1989–Nov. 7, 1990

YES, I want to win the Walt Disney World® vacation for two! I understand the prize includes round-trip airfare, first-class hotel, and a daily allowance as revealed on the "Wallet" scratch-off card.

Name____________________

Address____________________

City__________ State/Prov.______ Zip/Postal Code______

Daytime phone number____________________
Area code

Return entries with invoice in envelope provided. Each book in this shipment has two entry coupons—and the more coupons you enter, the better your chances of winning!

© 1989 HARLEQUIN ENTERPRISES LTD.

DINDL-1